ZOOM'S ACADEMY

ZOOM'S ACADEMY

WRITTEN AND ILLUSTRATED BY
JASON LETHCOE

BALLANTINE BOOKS NEW YORK

A Ballantine Books Trade Paperback Edition

Published in the United States by Ballantine Books,
an imprint of The Random House Publishing Group,
a division of Random House, Inc., New York.

Amazing Adventures from Zoom's Academy first published in the United States in a slightly different form by The Moon Factor in 2003, and subsequently published by Ballantine Books, an imprint of the Random House Publishing Group, a division of Random House, Inc., in 2005, in trade paperback.
Amazing Adventures from Zoom's Academy: The Capture of the Crimson Cape originally published in the United States by Ballantine Books, an imprint of the Random House Publishing Group, a division of Random House, Inc., in 2006, in trade paperback.

www.ballantinebooks.com

ISBN 0-345-49641-8

Printed in the United States of America

2 4 6 8 9 7 5 3 1

Book design by Joanne Yates Russell

AMAZING ADVENTURES

. . . from . . .

For Emily, who has superpowers and doesn't know it yet.

CONTENTS

CONTENTS

AMAZING ADVENTURES

. . . **from** . . .

...1 SUMMER

SUMMER did not want to wake up. She screwed her face up with concentration, attempting to muster up a quick stomachache so she wouldn't have to face another horrible day at Jefferson Junior High. As if her daily routine at the school wasn't bad enough, today she was supposed to play in a soccer game that she was thoroughly dreading. With both hands firmly resting on her forehead trying to warm it to fever temperature, she peeked out from beneath her rumpled bedcovers.

The hands on her *Gothic Girl* alarm clock pointed to 7:45 A.M. Arrgh . . . she could swear the hands moved faster on school mornings.

"Summer! Wake up, kiddo, you're gonna be late for school!" Her dad's baritone voice floated up from downstairs.

"I'm not going to go. I feel sick." Summer knew it was feeble but it was the best, and unfortunately, most overused excuse she could think of. She felt like she would do anything to get out of the soccer game that she was supposed to play in that afternoon.

Downstairs, Jasper, Summer's father, moved to the stove and retrieved a batch of gourmet pancakes. "Get a move on, the bus will be here any minute!"

Summer, with a reluctant sigh, threw off the bedcovers and shuffled to her nearby bathroom. Her fingers groped for the switch.

As the light clicked on, Summer gazed at her reflection in the medicine cabinet mirror with distaste. Nelson, her small tabby, watched from a stool near the sink as Summer made a perfunctory inspection of her facial features. "You don't have to worry about having a giant nose, too many freckles, and glasses. Be thankful you're a cat."

Nelson meowed sympathetically as Summer made a gagging gesture at her reflection, gave him a pat on the head, and turned on the shower. *Not to mention the fact that I'm probably the worst soccer player ever,* she thought miserably.

Her parents had divorced when she was six. The custody battle had been long and arduous. In the end, the agreement had been that her parents would split the time fifty-fifty. Summer never understood the reasons for the divorce, but loved them both. Fortunately, they never tried to get her to "take sides," but she constantly found herself frustrated and caught in the middle.

Her dad was eccentric, to put it mildly. He had a big picture of Thomas Edison in the living room and Summer even caught him talking to it once or twice when he didn't know she was looking. He was forever tinkering, hoping to make a monumental scientific breakthrough. Summer observed that almost everything he made backfired or exploded. In many pictures of her dad, he had used a grease pencil to stencil in his eyebrows because of the constant singeing they had been subjected to.

Her mom was the opposite. Queen of her legal firm, Jones, Bartholomew and Edwards, she represented herself in the divorce proceedings and practically reduced her dad's attorney to an ineffectual schoolboy. She was efficient, levelheaded, and persistent. A consummate pro.

When she was little, Summer had spent countless hours trying to imitate both of them, secretly hoping to ensure their love and approval through a carefully orchestrated performance. She realized soon enough that she couldn't maintain the facade, especially when she entered junior high.

Life at Jefferson was a constant struggle. She was reminded every day of how unpopular and geeky she was. She spent countless hours trying to figure out how to change her destined social status at school. This was the reason she signed up for the soccer team. She was terrible at sports, but hoped that by making the team, even though she was just an alternate, she might gain a few brownie points with her peers. Of course, it hadn't worked. She was as unpopular as ever, and a terrible soccer player to boot.

Dressed in her neatly pressed uniform, Summer went downstairs. Her dad was busy sprinkling candied pecans on top of a stack of perfectly browned pancakes. Summer noticed that he placed a very strange forklike contraption next to the two plates. Ignoring this, she plodded to the kitchen pantry, took out a box of Alpha-O's cereal, and slumped into her spot at the table.

"Honey, you're missing the opportunity to be the first to try my latest invention . . . a fork with a hydraulic attachment for regulating the flow of maple syrup over pancakes!"

Summer pretended not to hear as her father took the fork, positioned it over the stack of pancakes, and pushed the button. Nothing happened. He frowned and fiddled with the contraption.

"I can't figure out what could be wrong." Jasper shook the fork up and down and placed a searching eye next to the tiny spout.

Summer rolled her eyes. "Here it comes . . ." She had watched her dad struggle with his gadgets countless times before and could anticipate what was coming next. With a loud *glurk,* hot maple syrup shot out of the end of the fork, drenching both the table and Jasper in a sticky mess.

"Whoops!" Her dad struggled to control the sputtering device, fumbling with his sticky hands as the fork flew out of his fingers. It landed clattering on the kitchen floor, spraying out the last of its syrupy contents. Jasper, with practiced calmness, walked over and picked it up. While wiping the dripping syrup from his face with the back of his hand, he raised an analytical eyebrow at the device. "Hydraulic overload. Of course. Should have seen it. This will definitely mean further testing."

Summer groaned as he went to the kitchen sink and began to clean up. Why couldn't her dad at least *try* acting normal once in a while? *It's no wonder I have such problems trying to be cool,* Summer thought. She was convinced that all of the evidence pointed to the fact that she had inherited a major dose of "geek genes" from her dad. She scowled as she munched a couple of bites of the soggy cereal while Jasper filled the sink with bubbling soapy water.

"So, are you ready for the big soccer finals?"

Summer winced.

"Dad, I'm fourth string. I never play."

Jasper pulled his sticky fishing hat from the scalding water.

"I'm sure you will get your big chance today. I have a funny feeling about this game. Just wait and see, you're gonna do great!"

Summer forced a smile. It was always the same thing. Her dad was an optimist, constantly mentioning "silver linings" and stuff like that. Summer didn't believe life was that simple. When you are the most unpopular girl at Jefferson Junior High, "silver linings" were hard to come by.

She glanced down and noticed that the letters in her cereal bowl spelled out the word "L-O-S-E-R." She was certain her dad was wrong about everything.

...2 THE BIG GAME

THE sun shone overhead in a brilliant blue sky. Excitement was buzzing through the Jefferson stadium crowd like an electrical current. Parents watched the field eagerly, hoping that their son or daughter would get a chance to play. The last game of the year was against their longtime rivals, the Westlake Wolves, and the "friendly" game had taken on a fiercely competitive edge.

Summer sat in her usual spot on the bench, watching the other players. The score was tied, with only five minutes left.

She gazed up at the stands, which were jammed with students and family members, shouting for their favorite team. She caught sight of her dad, who was wearing two giant foam "We're Number One!" fingers, one on each hand, and was whistling shrilly through his teeth.

"I must have been adopted," she muttered underneath her breath, feeling completely embarrassed. She returned her concentration to the game.

Just when her team had been about to score, a Jefferson forward collided with Westlake's burly goalie. There was a sickening *crunch* as he collapsed underneath a pile of kicking legs. The coach yelled "time out!" as the injured player was forced to take the bench. The team doctor took a long look at the boy's leg, pronounced it broken, and ordered a stretcher to take him from the field. The crowd applauded politely as the boy was carried away.

The injuries mounted as the game turned more and more brutal for Jefferson. Summer fidgeted nervously as she watched each of their first- and second-string players emerge from the game with injuries. It seemed like the referees were always looking the other way when the Wolves took a cheap shot at the other players. She wondered if there had ever been a game she hadn't wanted to play in more than this one.

I could die out there, she thought, feeling a sudden surge of panic.

Tweeet! A referee's whistle sounded as once more a stretcher was brought to the field to carry off another player.

"Oh, no, not Julia!" Summer watched as Julia, the only player who was close to Summer's skill level, left the field. The game had to be pretty bad if either of them had been called off of the bench.

Summer's coach scanned the bench, his eyes filled with desperation, looking for another substitute. Now all of the other first-, second-, or third-string players who sat on the bench had bandaged sprains or leg casts. Only Summer, the sole fourth-stringer, was uninjured and available.

"Please don't pick me . . . please . . . don't!" Summer prayed to herself. She complained about never getting a chance to play, but most of that was just for show. The thought of actually getting on the field and humiliating herself in front of the entire school was terrifying!

The coach sighed.

"Summer, get in there!"

With a sinking feeling in the pit of her stomach, Summer obediently walked onto the field. Jasper cheered wildly! It was the first time he could ever remember seeing his daughter get a chance to play. He grabbed the shoulder of the father next to him and shouted, his voice echoing through his homemade megaphone, "That's my daughter out there! *Go, Summer!*"

Before she knew what was happening, Summer found that the ball had been passed to her. Her surge of panic was quickly suppressed as she began dribbling the ball downfield. Maybe months of practice would pay off! Maybe she wasn't as bad at this as she thought! Jasper cheered himself hoarse! She was just a few feet from the goal without an opponent in sight.

"Come on, girl, don't blow it," Summer nervously whispered to herself.

She kicked the ball as hard as she could, but watched with dismay as her foot flew wide, barely touching the ball. She panicked, trying to get control of the ball again.

Just as she was about to try another kick, a player from the other team rushed at Summer and tackled her to the ground with an incredible slide. Summer had seen him earlier in the game, and had heard her teammates mention that he was Westlake's star player. She groaned as she felt her glasses fly from her face. As the two players crashed to the ground, their bodies entangled like a pretzel. Summer's only thought was, *No, not my glasses!* She was practically blind without them.

After shaking off the initial shock, Summer grabbed the boy's shoulder to steady herself and began her blurry search. She was so intent on finding her glasses that she hardly noticed the strange tingling sensation that spread through her hand.

A puzzled expression came over the boy's face, whose shoulder she still held. He looked at Summer wonderingly for a moment, then gazed down at his legs in disbelief. Something weird was going on. His legs felt funny.

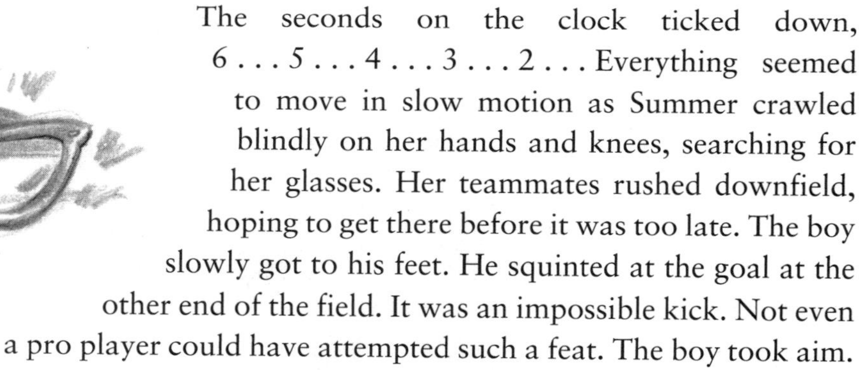

The seconds on the clock ticked down, 6 . . . 5 . . . 4 . . . 3 . . . 2 . . . Everything seemed to move in slow motion as Summer crawled blindly on her hands and knees, searching for her glasses. Her teammates rushed downfield, hoping to get there before it was too late. The boy slowly got to his feet. He squinted at the goal at the other end of the field. It was an impossible kick. Not even a pro player could have attempted such a feat. The boy took aim.

With a loud thump that sounded like a Mack truck hitting a two-ton mattress, the boy kicked the ball. It flew across the length of the field like a bullet and ripped through the net like it was made of spiderwebs. It was a miracle!

The entire crowd was stunned into silence. Nobody could believe what he or she had just witnessed! Summer retrieved her glasses in time to see the crowd shake itself from its stupor and leap to its feet with thunderous cheers. The only person not standing was Jasper, who stared down at Summer as though he had just seen a ghost.

Summer's teammates groaned. As they left the field, they threw insults at her, blaming her for the missed goal.

"Nice job, four-eyes!" Toby Parker pulled his hands up to his eyes, making the gesture of glasses. He then began awkwardly pretending to miss kicking the soccer ball. His teammates laughed at the imitation. Summer gathered up her gym bag and pretended not to notice.

"I hear that the other team wants to make her the team captain!"

With their mocking laughter echoing behind her, Summer sadly walked to her dad's beat-up VW Beetle that idled near the sidewalk. She opened the rusty door and slouched inside, unwilling to look her dad in the eye.

"I knew I would mess everything up," she whispered, her voice catching in her throat as the car rattled and smoked its way out of the school's parking lot.

...3 THE RING OF TRUTH

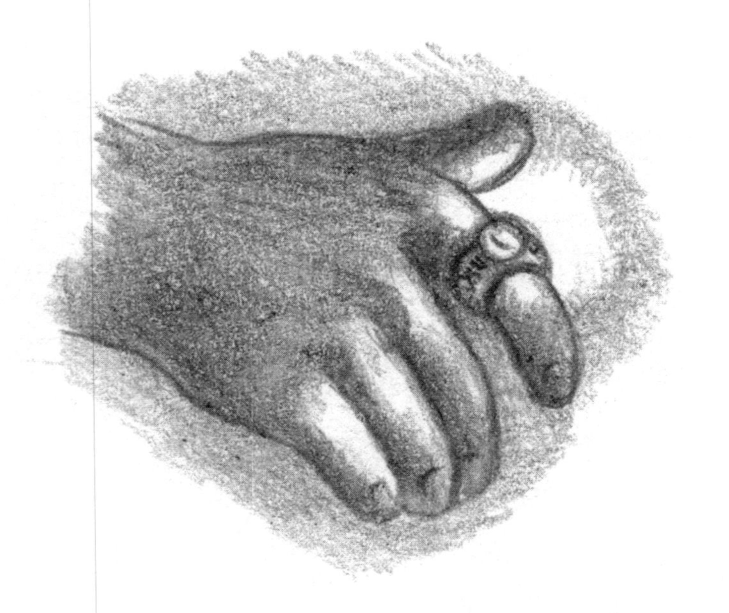

"WHAT do you mean I'm going to stay with you for the entire summer?" Summer wondered why her dad was acting so strange, even stranger than usual. Jasper paced nervously around the living room.

"I talked to your mom and she said it was fine under the circumstances. What I have to tell you may be, uh, well, hard to believe."

Summer's dad was now staring at the edge of his worn hat brim, distractedly trying to pick at a stray thread that was hanging down in front of his eyes.

"Dad, if you want to say something to me, just say it. I don't understand what the big deal is." Summer was getting frustrated with her dad. He had been really weird since the soccer game, flipping the TV on and off and muttering to himself constantly. She knew that whatever was going on had to be a pretty big deal, because her mom would rarely budge on the visitation schedule.

Jasper finally removed the thread and looked around conspiratorially. He motioned for Summer to sit down on the couch. Summer sat down and looked back expectantly. He sighed, and removed his hat for an instant to run a nervous hand through his thinning hair.

"Have you ever wondered why I have kept the name of the school where I teach a secret?"

Summer had always assumed that her dad taught at the local junior college. She shrugged. She couldn't understand what he was getting at. Undeterred, the fidgety Jasper continued.

"I am secretly an instructor at Zoom's Academy for the Super-Gifted." He waited for the effect of his words to sink in.

Summer stared back unimpressed.

"I'm serious, it's a school for the research and development of superpowers!"

Summer was waiting for the punch line. What was he talking about? Superpowers? Come on.

Jasper grabbed a stack of comic books and excitedly pointed to the covers. "These guys are all graduates!"

Summer gave her dad a look that plainly said that she thought that he was off his rocker. Jasper, however, wasn't finished.

"Look, I have had to bide my time, waiting for the right opportunity to test you to find out if you have any superabilities. I think what happened on the soccer field might have something to do with the supernatural."

Summer felt completely confused. Okay, fine then. If her dad wanted to play some "superhero game" she would go along with it.

Summer grinned at her dad and said, "Okay, Dad, whatever . . ."

Jasper walked over to an ancient-looking china cabinet in the dining room and opened the top drawer. He stretched his hand to the very back of the drawer and, with a grunt, retrieved a mysterious box.

Summer couldn't help feeling mildly impressed as he removed an ornately designed silver ring from the box. This was pretty good. If he had planned all of this, he had done a great job keeping it a secret from her.

Jasper stared at the ring with a momentary look of fear and wonder.

You've got to be kidding! How hokey could you get? Summer said playfully, "Don't tell me. That is the magical ring that gives the wearer special powers!" She had read plenty of sci-fi books.

Jasper chuckled nervously, then stared at Summer with an eager expression. "Not exactly. What we hope is that the ring will tell us if you have any superpowers inside of you. This moment could change your life forever."

Maybe it was the way he looked at her with such intensity, but Summer suddenly felt a twinge of uncertainty as her dad placed the heavy ring in her outstretched palm.

She stared at the ring for a moment. It looked like something from outer space. The metal was oddly transparent, and the crystalline stone that was set in the middle was white with an emblem of a Z with wings glittering inside of it. As she inspected it more closely, she noticed strange, alien letters etched across the band.

"This is really weird," Summer whispered.

She decided to try it on. Summer gasped as the ring immediately reduced in size to fit her finger perfectly. Her dad's eyes were focused on the ring with a sharp, intense stare.

Suddenly the ring began to hum. With a spark, it came to life and glowed with a small, steady bluish light. Summer almost fell off the couch with surprise! She felt a strange sensation, almost like the feeling when it's Christmas morning and you are the first one awake. She felt inexplicably happy!

She glanced over at her dad. He was making a funny coughing noise in his throat, pretending to inspect something on the couch. Summer could only remember seeing her dad cry once. She had spied on him late one night when he was looking at a photo album with old pictures of him and her mom from when they were still married. She had never forgotten how sad he looked that night. This time, when she looked up and saw tears in his eyes, it was different. He looked happier than she had ever seen him. He blinked the tears away self-consciously, and then looked out of the window. When he turned back to look at her he had a huge smile.

"You have no idea how long I've waited for this day to come! Are you ready to be totally freaked out?"

He gave her a wink, and got up from the couch. He moved a bit spasmodically, as if he was trying to control his excitement. Summer watched as he took the remote control for the TV and started punching buttons with a feverish intensity. The TV screen was momentarily black. Jasper entered a channel number somewhere in the thousands. With a tiny *blip*, a small cursor suddenly appeared. Jasper entered a numerical code.

Summer felt her face go slack with amazement as she watched the entertainment center she had seen a thousand times before suddenly rotate on its base and reveal a secret room! Two gleaming brass poles were inside, apparently leading down to hidden depths below the house. Her dad flashed a toothy grin at her stupefied expression.

"And you didn't believe me," he chided as he grabbed a pole and slid down. The last thing Summer heard was his voice floating up from below saying, "Last one down is a rotten egg!"

...4 BLAST OFF!

SUMMER hesitantly grasped the brass pole and slid down into darkness. She felt a strange sensation halfway through the speedy descent, almost like mechanical hands were pulling and pushing her along. When she reached the bottom she gazed around her new surroundings with awe.

She was in an immense underground cavern that was filled with blinking computer lights and strange contraptions. She looked down and was shocked to find that she was wearing bright orange spandex and a cape.

"Whoa," she whispered. "This is *really* strange."

She noticed that she was wearing an emblem on her chest. It was the same "Z" she had seen on the ring earlier.

"You will get your own symbol when you graduate." Her father's voice floated back to her out of the gloom. "I have had a costume ready for you for some time now. How does it fit?"

"Well," she replied, "it fits fine. I, uh, don't know about the color though." Summer frowned down at the neon-orange tights.

"Couldn't you have picked something, oh, I don't know, a little more conservative?"

Jasper emerged from a side cavern carrying an unusual-looking flashlight and chuckled. "Look, if you don't like it, you can work on your own design in Miss Powers's Costume Design class."

Summer noticed that he was wearing a gray costume with dark blue boots and gloves. His chest had an emblem of a large, old-fashioned, smiling moon on it, surrounded by a silver oval. He was still wearing his fishing hat, which, in Summer's estimation, kind of hurt the whole "crime-fighter" look.

"Um, Dad, where are we? Is all of this under our house or something?"

Jasper held out his hands in

an all-encompassing gesture. "This," he replied, "is our secret, high-tech crime-fighting headquarters. It's also where I commute to work from each morning."

Summer looked at her dad skeptically. "Wait a minute. I've seen you drive to work in the morning. Don't tell me that you always turned around and came back home after I caught the bus?"

"Yep, every morning for thirteen years."

Jasper grinned widely. Summer thought she must be dreaming. It was just too weird. Wordlessly, she walked forward as her dad motioned for her to follow him to a nearby cavern.

They walked over to an immense door. Jasper pressed his palm into a scanner and the huge metal door swung slowly open. Summer gasped. There, sitting on a launching pad, was a gigantic metal rocket. Steam was hissing from its base, and hoses were everywhere.

Summer noticed more retro-looking blinking computer lights flashing around the room. She was instantly reminded of those old fifties sci-fi movies with the rocket ships sliding down an inexpertly hidden wire and a lit sparkler giving the supposed effect of blasting through space.

"Can you believe that it actually runs on lime gelatin? I figured it out one day when I was conducting an experiment. I was upstairs in my den, and accidentally dropped my lunch into a vat of hydrochloric acid (dangerous stuff, hydrochloric acid), anyway, I reached in with a pair of tongs and discovered that the gelatin had somehow impossibly remained intact. I couldn't believe it. Upon further examination, however, I discovered that . . ."

"Dad! I am absolutely not going into that thing. This is totally crazy!" Summer pointed a quivering finger at the rocket.

"This is just . . . wrong. Very, very wrong." She began to back out of the room with a look of utter horror on her face.

"What, the rocket? Oh, honey, don't worry. I've installed all of the modern safety features. It even has air bags."

As if on cue, the rocket suddenly let out a huge hiss of steam and one of the blinking lights fell off. Summer wheeled angrily on Jasper.

"Dad, I'm not going to do it. I . . . I . . . can't. You know about my fear of heights!"

Jasper was tightening the screw that held the light in place. "I have already taken that into account." Jasper turned from the repositioned light and walked over to a nearby workbench. He lifted a glass astronaut helmet from the table and walked over to Summer.

"I really am proud of this. It not only works as a space helmet, but I installed a hypnotic device that puts the wearer safely and immediately to sleep. No anxiety, no motion sickness, nothing. You sleep, you wake up, boom!" He swept his hand quickly through the air. "You're there." Jasper beamed a proud smile at his daughter.

Summer took the helmet in her hands and gazed at the little silver box installed on its side. Her dad was brilliant, she knew that, but he was also prone to a few accidents now and then. She just didn't want this to be one of "those times."

"Okay, Dad. If you say so." Her lips tightened and she glared at Jasper. "But if this thing doesn't work . . . so help me!"

Jasper raised his hand like an oath and grinned. "I swear that it works. Don't worry, honey, it's gonna be great!"

Summer always had a hard time remembering the next few minutes when she recounted the story to her friends later. She remembered her dad preparing for takeoff, getting a picnic basket out of the fridge, and mentioning something about having forgotten to buy some extra chocolate chip cookies.

She could foggily recall being strapped into a seat that looked straight up through a small window. As her dad fastened the helmet and turned on the hypnotic device, she heard beautiful music and started to feel really sleepy.

The last thing she could recall was smiling at the thought of her dad pulling out his keys from his pocket and starting the rocket up as if it were a Volkswagen. There was a loud roar, some doors opened in the ceiling, and what felt like a heavy blanket pushed down against her chest. After that, everything was black.

...5 THE FIGURE

In the deepest part of the Pacific Ocean, giant sharks circled the gothic-looking underwater castle that crouched menacingly underneath a glowing dome of greenish glass. Inside a tall tower, a brooding, shadowy figure stared out of the window at the restless predator fish from his ornately carved bedside. Pure malevolence radiated from the figure's soulless eyes.

A tentative knock on the chamber door interrupted his reverie. The door slowly creaked open to reveal an exceptionally nervous young boy wearing a skull-like mask and a tattered cape.

"Excuse me, sir, but word has arrived that Captain Truehart has been officially declared dead."

The figure remained motionless.

"I hope you are feeling better, sir?"

The figure's eyes glittered in the darkness.

"I will recover," he said menacingly.

The boy was feeling a little bolder because of his answered questions.

"It's too bad that your brother isn't around anymore. I'm sure he could have probably helped to heal you."

The figure on the bed let out a scorching hiss.

A look of fear crossed the boy's face.

"I . . . I'm sorry, sir . . . I didn't mean . . ."

The figure turned his head to face the stammering boy, illuminating a horribly distorted face. The boy recoiled as the figure's fearsome shadow loomed across the green-lit wall.

"You will never mention my brother in my presence again," he whispered. "If you do, I will arrange the most terrible punishment you can imagine. Now, LEAVE ME!"

The shaking boy made a hurried bow, and rushed from the darkened chamber.

...6 ZOOM'S ACADEMY

THE next thing Summer knew, her dad was shouting for her to wake up. "We're here! Look out the window!"

Summer felt as if she had been sleeping for a week. Groggily, she opened her eyes and yawned. What she saw outside the spaceship window made her jump with surprise! A flash of crimson shot past her window followed by three more figures in capes on a strafing flyby.

Summer struggled to say something but the words caught in her throat.

"They're . . . they're . . ."

". . . They're flying," finished Jasper. "I know, pretty cool, huh?"

Summer was speechless.

A girl about Summer's age, dressed in burgundy and wearing a hooded cape, flew up alongside Summer's window. Summer's face must have had a totally "gawked-out" expression on it, because the girl looked at her and laughed. She waved at Jasper, who waved back.

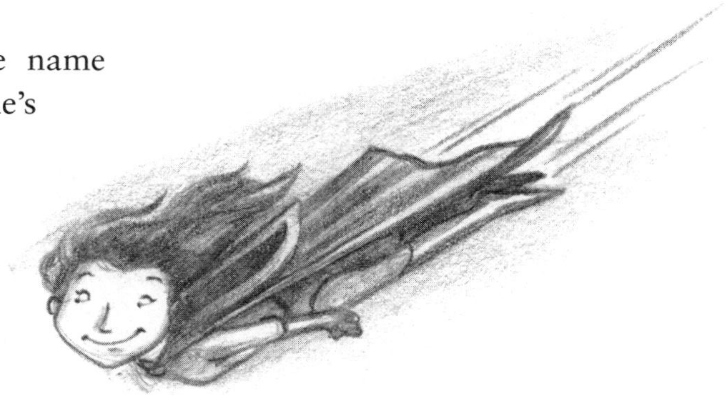

"That's Stephanie. She goes by the name 'Ruby Avenger' while she is at Zoom's. She's in my homeroom," explained Jasper.

Stephanie showed off some of her best aerial stunts, and then rejoined the others as they looped and dove on their way back to the school.

"If you look outside and to the right you will see it coming up on your side."

Her dad banked the rocket and Summer got her first glimpse of Zoom's Academy. It looked like an island floating in the sky surrounded by clouds. Retro space-styled buildings pointed toward the heavens at odd jutting angles. A giant orb with a glittering "Z" hovered over what appeared to be the central building on campus, a towering structure that reminded Summer of the Goodyear blimp set on its side. Young students in brightly colored superhero outfits soared across the sky, practicing their flying techniques.

Summer was so mesmerized by the spectacle that she momentarily forgot about her paralyzing fear of heights. She made the mistake of looking down. She could see the curve of the planet stretching off into the horizon. They were almost out of the atmosphere!

"Yaaaagh! Dad, turn on the hypno-thingy!" Summer felt queasy and her vision started to blur.

Her dad punched a button on the console. "Ooops! I guess it malfunctioned! Hang on, kiddo, we're about to land." Summer kept her eyes tightly closed as the rocket made its approach and was landed by her dad. There was a huge bump, and then the sound of pressurized steam being released by a series of automatic valves.

"You can open your eyes now, we're here."

Summer cracked open her eyes and saw her dad busily unbuckle his safety harness and release the air lock. Cool, fresh air rushed into the cabin.

Summer was practically stepping on Jasper's head in her eagerness to get out of the rocket and down the ladder after him.

When they had both reached the ground, Jasper unloaded their suitcases from a hidden compartment on the side of the rocket. Summer was reaching for her purple overnight bag when suddenly a mechanical voice made them freeze and turn around.

"*Bzzzt. Click.* Identification, please." The voice came from one of several shiny brass robots.

Their faces looked friendly, each of them wore a tin-plated

handlebar mustache, but they were holding ray gun-styled weapons and their voices didn't sound welcoming.

"Hold on a minute, let me get my wallet." Jasper reached into his pocket and produced his faculty ID. "There is never this kind of security. Something must have happened." Jasper's whisper sounded concerned.

The contraption in charge took the badge and scanned it with his finger. After approving the ID badge, the robot returned it to Jasper and rattled an apology.

"*Bzzt. Whirr. Click.* I'm sorry for the inconvenience, Mr. Jones. Is this your daughter?" The machine indicated Summer with a nod.

"Yes," said Jasper. "Please list her as a new student in your records, her name is Summer."

"Welcome to Zoom's Academy, Summer Jones," the entire squad greeted her in unison.

Summer smiled awkwardly and said, "Thanks."

The commanding robot issued marching orders and after a quick salute to her dad, they marched back to their patrol.

Jasper scratched his head. "Wonder what that was all about. Oh, well, guess we'll find out soon enough. Come on, kiddo, follow me."

Summer followed her dad to a machine that transmitted their luggage via particle transmission to their respective quarters. Summer was amazed to see her luggage get scanned by a laser beam and then disappear. A receipt printed out with a small map on the back for locating her luggage at the student dormitories.

"Wow, Dad, it says here that the dorm room is up in a big tree!" Summer was scanning the map and noticed that the picture of the student dorm rooms looked like the tree house from *The Swiss Family Robinson.*

"You are gonna love it. It's got ladders to rooms all over the branches. The thing is huge! You ought to see it at night . . . all lit up. It's amazing."

Summer noticed that they had arrived at a hovering stairway that led up to a booth floating fifty feet in the air. The booth was supported by an enormous multicolored patchwork zeppelin. Summer could make out other new students ascending to the top and receiving what looked like old-fashioned propeller beanies.

When they tweaked the prop, they flew into the air off of the floating platform and made their way to various destinations at the school.

"Dad?"

"Yes?"

"Do you mind if we just walk to wherever we're going?" Summer could only imagine how badly her fear of heights would affect her flying around with one of those things on. Her palms started to sweat and she felt nauseous just thinking about it.

Jasper paused as he was about to ascend the platform.

"Oh." He looked disappointed. "Are you sure? Principal Zoom designed them for the new students who haven't learned how to fly yet. They really are safe; they stick to your head until you tell them to let you go."

Summer didn't want to disappoint him.

"Dad, I'll do it if you want me to. But I feel like I might be sick if I went up in one of those things."

Jasper glanced up the stairway. A boy about Summer's age let out a whoop of delight as he took off into the air. Jasper turned back to Summer with a compassionate smile. He knew that she suffered from some pretty big anxieties, and didn't want to make her feel too pressured.

"Hey, they're not that great anyway . . . the walk will do us good."

Jasper and Summer walked down the stairs to a series of moving sidewalks that moved much slower than the beanies, but still offered an amazing view of the campus.

Her dad pointed at the tall blimplike tower with the "Z" above it.

"That's the Administration Building. Principal Zoom has his office on the top floor. The 1,447th floor to be exact."

Summer gazed up at the towering edifice with awe.

"Dad, what's he like? Principal Zoom, I mean."

Jasper lit his pipe, and puffed thoughtfully. "Well, he had tremendous power. That's just for starters. His race saw the potential to save Earth from destroying itself and started the search for people with heroic powers."

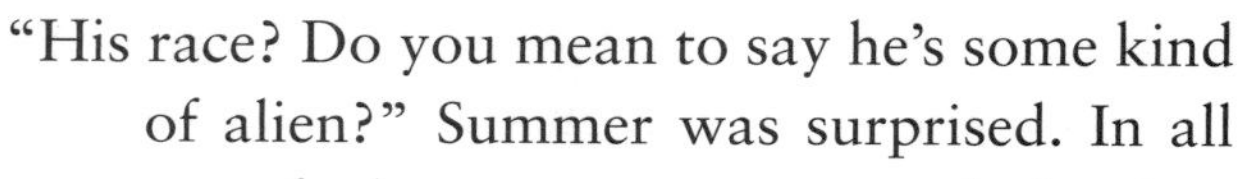

"His race? Do you mean to say he's some kind of alien?" Summer was surprised. In all of the strange events of the last twenty-four hours, she had never even considered the possibility of alien life-forms at the school. She imagined a bulbous-headed sticklike little creature with impenetrable, black, almond-shaped eyes. The image gave her the shivers.

"Yes, he's an alien. But probably not what you might expect him to look like."

They chatted as the side-walk rolled gently along, finally rounding a bend where Sum-mer was startled to see odd-looking buildings poking up over the trees. She thought that they looked as if they were made out of pillows. "I haven't been over here in ages," said Jasper with a grin. "Welcome to Sof' City! It is an entire city made of inflatable skyscrapers and cars for young heroes to practice in."

Summer spotted a girl with a pink cape lift an inflatable school bus above her head and send it flying across a street at an awaiting boy who caught it in midair, laughing.

The moving sidewalk made a sloping left turn and Summer found herself looking up at a structure that resembled a giant, silver marshmallow.

She followed her dad through a transparent purplish door made of some kind of ooze. When they emerged on the other side, Summer found that her feet bounced as they walked on the spongy street.

"Now this I can handle!" Summer said happily as she made a small jump, and bounced several inches off of the ground.

Jasper grinned, watching the hordes of Zoom's students bounce around the city, ricocheting off of the buildings with wild abandon. "The city is filled with all kinds of fun things to do. Many of the students come here on their off hours to try out some of the new missions that Foggleberry comes up with to help them test their new powers."

Summer looked up at him quizzically. "What's a Fuggleberry?"

"Foggleberry," her father corrected. "He's the little guy who comes up with all kinds of simulated events in the city. Bank robberies, villains trying to take over the city, you know, the typical stuff from comic books . . . *Whoops!*" Jasper ducked as an inflatable lamppost sailed right next to his head and knocked his hat off. "Sorry, Mr. Jones!" Summer stared openmouthed as she watched a girl who was standing a block away stretch two incredibly long arms over their heads and retrieve the streetlamp with one hand and her dad's hat with the other.

"Don't worry about it, Bungee Girl." The girl, whose arms had returned to normal, blushed and ran back to rejoin her friends down the street.

"Dad, this is really going to take some getting used to," Summer mused as she continued to stare after the girl. Jasper chuckled.

"I know it's a little crazy and hard to believe at first. But you'll get used to it." He held up his hand as if signaling for a taxi. Suddenly a little yellow cab, pillowy like everything else, pulled up next to them.

"Captain Creampuff's Bakery, please."

Summer had barely closed the door when the cab shot off like a roller coaster and ascended seven floors to their destination building.

Summer breathed a sigh of relief when they arrived. *Sheesh, did everything here at Zoom's require going up into the sky?* She stepped out of the car while it hovered alongside of a small bridge, and clung to the rail as her dad deposited a triangular coin into it. The car dinged appreciatively, and shot off to find its next fare.

"What does it use the money for?" Summer and her dad walked across the high platform to the entrance of the magnificent-looking bakery.

"It eats it," Jasper replied simply. A frumpy, gum-smacking robot waitress seated Summer and Jasper inside the restaurant.

"What'll it be, sweetie?" She indicated Summer with a bored tilt of her head.

Summer was so amazed by the robot's lifelike manner that she forgot to look at the menu. Her dad suggested Dr. Lightwave's Power Punch and a Marvelous Mega Muffin for Summer, and a Soy Latte for himself.

As the waitress rolled away with their order, Summer's eyes absorbed the space-age bakery's decor. Little robot birds with blue lights in their bellies twittered and chirped as they flew around the ceiling, illuminating the restaurant. The walls seemed to be made of something that looked like silver honeycomb. The hexagons that made up the walls shifted constantly, revealing little metal doors that opened and closed, displaying the customers' order choices.

When Summer's order came up, a box-shaped robot scurried across the floor, extended a long arm to retrieve it, then zipped back to their table and expertly placed the plate and drink in front of her. Summer sipped the drink suspiciously from the glowing, smoking beaker.

"Well, what do you think?" her dad asked.

"Mmmmmmm!" Summer, no longer reticent, slurped the drink noisily and with great gulps. It was the best thing she had ever tasted. Sort of a strawberry-boysenberry concoction, with a little kick of something else . . . something that Summer couldn't identify but that made the little hairs on her arms tingle.

"Take it easy! They don't call it 'Power Punch' for nothing!" Jasper smiled at his daughter, who had a pink mustache on her upper lip.

"What do you mean?" asked Summer.

"Well, it's just that it does exactly what the name says. I saw one kid accidentally punch a hole the size of a trash-can lid through one of the tables. Had to do dishes here for a month to pay for it."

Summer decided that she had better put the drink down for now; her arms were already vibrating with unbelievable strength! She felt as if she could punch through solid steel if she wanted to.

"Don't worry, it only lasts for about five seconds." Jasper chuckled. "It is the closest thing we have here at the Academy to a superpower enhancer."

Summer looked at her dad questioningly.

Jasper leaned forward.

"You see, here at Zoom's we have scientists working around the clock to try to find a way to make the heroes' powers stronger. The war with the supervillains never rests. Each side is always trying to get the edge on the other."

Jasper paused thoughtfully. "It's terrible, really. The biggest problem with the war is that the villains never fight fair. They are always coming up with evil plans that will destroy entire continents! Most of the supervillains are crazy. They never seem to know when to stop." A cloud passed over Jasper's face.

Summer thought about all of the villains in comic books and movies. It was fun to read and watch them when it wasn't real. But this was totally different. They seemed much more frightening when she thought of people in outrageous costumes threatening to take over the world in real life! She fiddled awkwardly with her straw, feeling nervous.

The waitress brought the bill. Jasper dug in his pockets for a couple of the strange coins.

"Dad?"

"Yeah."

"What happens to the students after they graduate? Where do they go?"

Jasper placed the coins next to the bill and got up from the table. "Well, most go on to form special leagues, secret societies . . . you know. The rest, well, they go on to join the New York Fire Department."

Jasper gave his daughter a playful wink as they stepped outside the bakery and into the mall.

"Okay, here are some Zoom bucks." Jasper placed a small handful of coins of different sizes and shapes into Summer's hand.

"Go see Foggleberry. He will come up with a simulated mission for you to do. You'll love it; it's like being in a big video game. I will meet you in, say, an hour?"

Summer agreed. She felt excited! She liked to play computer games back home, but she suspected that this was going to be ten times more fun! She decided to walk to the shop, not wanting another flying experience in one of those pillowy taxis. She had gotten the hang of gliding her way around, and after a brief inspection of the city directory, she floated up a walkway covered with a twisting fish motif to the outside of the strangest-looking building she had ever seen.

. . . 7

FOGGLEBERRY'S

IT wasn't that the outside looked like anything special. It was primarily black, with a very small sign on the door that simply said "*Foggleberry's*" in neatly painted silver letters. It was when Summer opened the door that she received the shock. It was like walking around inside of a lava lamp. Hundreds of huge red and blue blobs made from some kind of amorphous material floated in the air with cubelike displays of the latest superhero technology resting on the blobs' tensile surfaces.

Shoppers were given long hooks and allowed to roam through the gift shop, catching whatever item they wanted to see. Summer thought it looked like people with shepherd hooks trying to capture clouds.

Suddenly a noise that sounded like oatmeal being blown through a kazoo startled her out of her thoughts. She looked down to see a strange short man in a yellow top hat wiping his red bulbous nose with a spotted handkerchief. He couldn't have been more than three feet tall.

In a stuffy voice he said, "Are you a dew dewdent or ab bisitor?" Summer was confused by the man's strange speech.

"I'm sorry . . . what?"

"Are you a dew dewdent or ab bisitor?" The little man sounded very annoyed.

"Oh . . . you mean a new student or a visitor?"

"Dat's what Ib sayink, a dew dewdent or ab bisitor." The little man sneezed into his handkerchief, making the awful noise again. Summer quickly replied that she was a new student.

"I'b sorry about by dose. Terrible allergies." The little man took her arm and guided her toward an area that had long lines of kids waiting their turn to go inside of what looked like a dark cave.

"This is the dew dewdent simulation. You will be gibben indructions inside. Hab a great time, and don't be derbous." He glanced at the expression on Summer's face and smiled reassuringly. Summer nodded and stepped in line.

Summer looked around the room. Kids were everywhere, arguing about who had the high score on different missions. Displays containing X-ray glasses and telepathy helmets hovered throughout the souvenir shop. She spotted a blob floating by containing postcards with colorful pictures of Zoom's printed on them. She was just thinking about how she would like to send one to her mom when a loud commotion nearby caught her attention. There, next to a display of winged boots, was a handsome boy resplendent in a heroic blue and red uniform being mobbed by a crowd of students.

"Hey, Tommy, show us the Truehart Twist!" a voice shouted.

Tommy, his strong chin lifted in an arrogant way, said, "You've got to be kidding! That maneuver my dad made up is so old school. I do things now that even he never dreamed of."

Summer walked over to the crowd to see what was going on. The young boy was certainly handsome enough. Summer felt her heart beat a little faster when she saw his eyes briefly glance in her direction.

Another voice yelled out, "Give us a demo, man. Come on . . . show us your stuff!"

Tommy let out an exasperated sigh and motioned for everyone to move back.

"Okay. Fine. Everybody move back, this is gonna be some 'hot stuff' so anybody who doesn't wanna get burned better move."

Instead of moving, the eager crowd pressed forward, with everyone jostling for a better look at what the young Truehart was capable of. Tommy's face darkened with irritation.

"I SAID MOVE BACK!" He roughly pushed several students out of the way, sending one smaller student sprawling into a blob that held a spinner rack full of comic books.

"Hey! Watch it, you big jerk!" The younger student jumped to his feet and rubbed his elbow with an angry look on his face. Tommy turned around slowly to face the younger boy.

The boy, who was dressed in a lime-green outfit and a winged helmet, stared defiantly back at Tommy. Summer had to give him credit. She thought that there weren't many students who would want to tangle with this kid. There was something that felt kind of dangerous about him in spite of his heroic colors. Tommy smiled with a cruel glint in his eye and took the boy by the collar.

"Look, everyone, it's Thunderclap Collins! The fastest thing on two legs."

Thunderclap squirmed nervously under the bigger boy's iron grip. Summer wondered if she should run to get some help. Tommy raised his hand. There was a hiss of something that sounded like a stove heating up, and then Tommy's fist suddenly burst into flame.

"Maybe this will help you set another speed record, huh, punk?"

Cries of "Fight! Fight!" echoed through the throng. The crowd pressed in for a better look. Summer was pushed from behind, and found herself jostled directly into Tommy.

Tommy whipped his head around. Summer panicked.

"I . . . I'm sorry, I didn't mean to . . ." But she never finished her sentence. At that moment huge beads of sweat started trickling down Tommy's face. He gasped, eyes bulging. The crowd began to murmur. Suddenly smoke shot out of his ears! The students scattered, many of them shouting and pointing at Tommy, whose rear end was on fire!

The sound of a crashing gong split the air. Flying down through the roof on silver-winged chariots was a team of heroic faculty members. A caped man with a crimson mask and pirate costume called for everyone to "Stand back!" He removed a small box with the name "T. Truehart" engraved on its top from inside of his chariot.

A loud hiss emitted as the box was opened. The man reached inside and pulled out a container marked "Snow from Jupiter's Moon."

Suddenly a raging blizzard of snow and ice came rushing out of the box to put out the flames. Tommy, his body racked with convulsions, staggered under the onslaught, then fainted. The two wings of the chariot separated from the wagon and re-formed into a silver sphere that lifted Tommy into the air and quickly took the unconscious boy to the nurse's office. The man in the crimson mask cast a grave expression on Summer and Thunderclap.

"I don't know exactly what this was all about." He looked around disapprovingly. "But no student at Zoom's is allowed to use his or her powers to harm another."

Summer felt like crawling underneath the floor. Thunderclap was still pale and a little shaky from the encounter with Tommy, and tried to look elsewhere.

"Arrr, what did ye do to Tommy Truehart to cause him to burst into flames like that?" The man stared at Summer with a mixture of curiosity and concern. Summer stared back blankly.

"I don't know. I didn't know that I did anything!" Summer felt the gazes of everyone in the shop upon her. It felt almost as bad as the time she blew it at the soccer game.

"Ye must be tested as soon as possible to determine what your superpowers be. I want ye to report to Principal Zoom's office immediately."

The other faculty members cast stern looks at Summer and departed. Summer was about to leave the store when she felt a heavy hand on her shoulder. She turned and saw a tall boy wearing a broad-brimmed hat that obscured his face looming behind her.

Before Summer could say anything he whispered something in her ear. He then turned his face toward the ceiling, shouted a strange word that sounded like "Crazakatha!" and shot into the air like a rocket, his cape fluttering behind him.

Thunderclap caught up to her, his voice sounding a little shaken. "Wow, I haven't heard that one yet. Amazing. I would have run out of them a long time ago."

Summer turned to Thunderclap, who was now staring up after the departing figure. "Run out of what?" asked Summer.

"That," explained Thunderclap, "is the Mysterious Snazzoo. He's really cool, very secretive. He has the power of the word."

Summer was confused. "What word?"

"He has to make up new words to activate his powers. It can be almost anything! But . . ." Thunderclap lowered his voice, "they say his weakness is that if he ever repeats himself, saying the same word more than once, he will explode on the spot! Poof! Kaboom! Gone!" Thunderclap zipped his hand through the air for emphasis.

Thunderclap opened the door out to the city for Summer and then followed.

"What is doubly weird is that he never knows what his power will be next. I guess it kinda depends on which word he makes up. All I know is that I would have run out of ideas for new words a long time ago. I'd pretty much be burnt toast by now." He chuckled.

"Snazzoo whispered something to me that made no sense," said Summer. Thunderclap whistled through his teeth. "Wow. He gave you one! Man, you are so lucky!"

"Well, I don't really know if it was a 'word' or not, all he said was . . ."

But before she could finish, Thunderclap covered her mouth and made shushing noises.

"Don't! If you say it now you'll waste it! Just memorize it . . . never write it down or it won't work anymore. Only use it when you really need it."

"But," said Summer, "if I don't know what it will do, then how do I know it will be something I want to happen anyway? Seems kind of silly to me."

Thunderclap shrugged. “All I know is that he hardly ever does that and he wouldn’t have done it if there wasn’t some reason. Maybe he wanted to help you.”

They walked comfortably side by side, a definite spring in their step as they bounced gently upon the city streets. Summer liked him. He was really easy to talk to and she felt like she could use a friend right now.

“My name is Summer Jones.”

Summer stretched out her hand. Thunderclap smiled warmly and shook it.

“I know. Your dad is probably my favorite teacher. He mentions you from time to time in his class. My real name is Archie, but around here I’m known as Thunderclap.”

...8 PRINCIPAL ZOOM

SUMMER and Thunderclap sat down on some benches to wait for Summer's dad. They chatted happily for a while, enjoying each other's company.

"So, what *is* the deal with Tommy Truehart anyway? Why has he got such a bad attitude?"

Thunderclap pondered Summer's question before replying.

"Well, I guess it's because his dad, Captain Truehart, died defending Zoom's from the head of our rival school, Graves Academy for the Villainous Arts. Everyone believes that Tommy will follow in his father's footsteps, becoming as great as he was."

Summer was intrigued by the notion of a villain school. She wondered if it was an amazing place like Zoom's was.

"Where is the villains' school? Does it float up in the sky too?"

Thunderclap was about to answer, but a ringing alarm caused him to look at his watch instead.

"Oh, man, I gotta get to the track! Mr. Fleet is gonna kill me! Listen, why don't we meet at the dorms later? I'll tell you all about it."

Summer had barely said "Okay" when Thunderclap's metal wings lifted on his helmet, pointing at the sky. The sky turned dark and an ugly-looking storm cloud came racing over the horizon. Thunderclap gazed upward for a minute, mumbling to himself.

Suddenly a bolt of lightning sizzled across the sky, striking Thunderclap's helmet. He yelped, rattling with the shock, then as the thunder boomed behind him he took off running. Summer had never seen anyone run so fast in her life! He was practically a blur! She was staring after him as her father walked up behind her.

"Now if only I could get him to be that punctual in my class . . ."

Summer stopped staring at Thunderclap and looked up at her dad. He smiled down at her with a twinkle in his eye.

"So, how did you like Foggleberry's, did you do good on the first mission?"

"Well no, I never actually got to try it." Summer fidgeted uncomfortably. "Something kind of bad happened when I was in there." She went on to relate all that had happened with Tommy Truehart. When she finished, Jasper told her who the man in the crimson mask and pirate garb was. He was a teacher named "Buccaneer" and assigned to Rescue Operations at Zoom's.

"We had better do as he says," said Jasper, "a renegade student with unknown powers can be dangerous to everyone."

"His pirate accent was kind of cheesy."

Jasper laughed.

"His real name is Bob Henderson and he's an accountant. When he discovered his superpowers, he really ran with the whole idea. I guess his life was pretty boring up until that point."

They walked outside the city, and back to the moving sidewalks. Soon they arrived at the Administration Building that Summer had seen from the rocket's window when they had approached Zoom's. She craned her neck back to try to see the top of it, making out the huge sphere with the glittering "Z" that hovered miles into the air.

The elevator mechanically announced that they had arrived at the 1,447th floor. The doors opened to reveal a magnificent reception area, decorated with immense statues of some of the most famous Zoom graduates. Summer followed her dad to an ornately designed robotic couch to wait for Principal Zoom.

She felt nervous. She had been sent to the principal's office once when she was in fourth grade. A few girls on the playground had decided to hide a jar of crickets inside of their teacher's desk. Summer happened to walk by when they were doing it, and when the teacher arrived on the scene she assumed that Summer was involved. She had straightened it out later, but remembered the panicky feeling in the pit of her stomach when it happened. She felt the same way now.

"Diet cola with lemon and a Captain Cranium." Summer looked over to see what her dad was doing. A panel slid back in the arm of the couch and an arm extended, revealing the soft drink and a comic book on a tray.

"Do you want anything while we wait?" Jasper asked. Summer shook her head. She was feeling too nervous. Jasper smiled encouragingly at Summer. "Relax. Principal Zoom will sort everything out."

Just then, a bell-like feminine voice from the couch said, "Principal Zoom will see you now."

Jasper and Summer stood up as two gilded mahogany doors swung open to reveal the professor.

Summer couldn't help smiling when she saw him. He was about three and a half feet tall, had a short elephant type of trunk, wispy gray hair, and a pair of aviator goggles perched neatly on the top of his head. All in all he looked friendly.

"Come in, come in," said the diminutive professor as he held out his three-fingered hands in welcome.

Summer and Jasper walked into his sumptuous office, which was covered from floor to ceiling with the heads of strange creatures mounted on the walls.

"Ah . . . you are wondering about my trophies?" Principal Zoom chuckled, a light fluty sound. "Welcome to the Wall of Heads."

Summer gazed around with a look of horror mixed with curiosity. Suddenly all of the heads in the room turned and looked at her with their beady black eyes. It was all she could do to stifle a scream!

The professor seemed amused. "Go ahead and give one of them a pat on the head."

Summer looked nervously at her dad, who lit his pipe and motioned for her to do what Principal Zoom had said.

Summer walked over to the least ferocious creature she could find. It looked like a cross between a rabbit and a bird, only its skin was covered in pink fur. She reached out a tentative hand to pat it. It was soft.

"Eggs, butter, and chocolate chip cookies." The creature shuddered to life and was speaking! Summer jumped back in surprise.

"And don't forget about the comic book convention on Neptune this weekend, you know how absentminded you get."

Principal Zoom cleared his throat.

"Don't worry, Loretta, I won't forget." The creature shot Principal Zoom a surly look and then resumed its previously frozen position.

Summer was amazed. "It isn't dead?"

"Actually, it isn't dead or alive at all. These are three-dimensional holograms of some of the more interesting creatures I have met on my travels. They look and feel real to the touch, but, I assure you, the owners of these heads would be quite disagreeable if they found out that their heads were really missing."

Principal Zoom walked over to a far wall where there was, remarkably, a head that looked just like Summer's favorite pop star, Eddie Fender. Zoom gave it a quick tap and it sparked to life, singing Summer's favorite song.

"Eddie is an old friend, and an ex-student. He always wanted to be on display here, so I obliged." Summer stared at the head in disbelief.

Principal Zoom chuckled again and disappeared for a moment behind his immense desk. When he reappeared, he was sitting on a high chair. "Please sit down, I already know what happened at Foggleberry's."

To Summer's intense relief, Principal Zoom knew that the whole event had been an accident.

"What we don't know is what exactly happened to Tommy; why his powers were suddenly out of control."

The professor removed his goggles and began polishing them with a small cloth.

"Tommy is haunted by his father's legacy, and is probably under a lot of emotional strain." The professor placed the goggles back on his nose and continued.

"Since Captain Truehart's recent death, the school has been under emergency watch, anticipating an attack from Graves Academy at any time."

Jasper glanced up suddenly. He and Principal Zoom exchanged a long look.

"Truehart was a good man, a real hero. He's going to be hard to replace." Zoom looked over at Summer and sighed.

"I'm very sorry that you are starting your schooling at Zoom's under such trying circumstances, but we will just have to make the best of it. Our first order of business is to have you tested."

He waggled a stubby finger at her. "Get lots of rest tonight. The testing you will go through in the morning will be very grueling." He smiled at Summer in a funny way that wrinkled his trunk.

Summer smiled back weakly. "Grueling"? What did he mean by "grueling"?

...9 THE TWO BROTHERS

SUMMER gazed outside the window of her room, which was nestled in the branches of the immense tree that housed all the students at Zoom's. The view was spectacular! The illuminated windows of little cottages set in the branches shone softly in the evening, reminding her of lit candles on a Christmas tree. Happy voices laughed and chatted as the students swung from benchlike swings high in the air, or climbed the rope ladders that led to their rooms.

Although she felt a little concerned about the testing process waiting for her in the morning, it was hard to feel anything but a wonderful sense of peace and happiness while staring outside at the beautiful starry night.

A knock at the door startled her out of her trance. She walked across the highly polished pine floor and opened the door. Thunderclap stood there smiling at her.

"Are you ready?"

"Sure, just give me a second to get my coat."

Although it was early June, the weather high up in the clouds was a little chilly at night. She went to her closet and pulled out an academy sweatshirt with the Zoom's logo emblazoned on the front.

"Okay . . . let's go."

Thunderclap led Summer up several ladders to a secret flat in the highest branches. When they climbed up, Summer could feel the mighty tree sway gently in the breeze. Her old fear of heights was sneaking up on her.

"Uh . . . Thunderclap, I don't know if I mentioned that I am afraid of heights." Summer's hands were searching for something on the floor that she could hold on to.

"Don't worry," said Archie, "there is a force field surrounding the tree. Watch!"

Summer looked around anxiously, hoping to see some indication of the field that Thunderclap had mentioned. Thunderclap demonstrated the force field by running to the end of the platform and jumping into the air. Summer noticed that instead of falling, he levitated in midair for a moment, then settled gently back to the ground. She felt very relieved.

He sat down beside her. "Okay then, you wanted to know about the villains' school, right?" Summer nodded. Thunderclap pulled out a small mechanical device. He flipped a tiny switch and with a crackle of electricity, a glowing orb appeared in the machine's center.

"This is a Holotron. It's kind of like a TV, but the main difference is that everything is in 3-D." The orb spun slowly in a circle, its weird purple light casting strange shadows in the treetops.

Summer listened with wide eyes as Thunderclap launched into the story about how Graves Academy came to be. The orb grew in size, and Summer could make out the images of two boys in scout uniforms walking carefully along the side of a rickety railroad trestle bridge. The boys looked down apprehensively at a dark river of rushing water cascading beneath it.

"There were a couple of brothers on their way home from a scout meeting. The story goes that one of them suggested a shortcut because they were so late."

The boys shared nervous glances as they made their way tentatively across the bridge. Suddenly, emerging silently out of the darkness, a group of tough-looking teenage thugs blocked the boys' progress.

"They didn't know that they were trespassing on the turf of a local street gang."

The gang began harassing the boys, picking up the younger brother and holding him by his ankles over the dangerous water. The older brother shouted for the bully to leave his brother alone. The bully sneered and threatened to drop him. The younger brother began to whimper.

"Sometimes when a kid first discovers that he has superpowers it happens when he feels helpless or angry."

The older brother clenched his fist as he watched his brother being tormented by the bully. He shouted for the bully to stop.

Summer watched the terrible scene as the younger brother struggled. Suddenly the bully lost his grip! The younger brother fell, disappearing into the misty fog below.

A blazing green light began building in the older brother's eyes. His whole body began to change, morphing into a fearsome, otherworldly beast with fangs.

"He wanted to do something terrible to the bullies. Something that would make them pay."

The brother lashed out with a clawed fist, sending a terrified bully crashing into a steel girder. He roared with an unearthly bellow.

Summer was horrified. "What happened to the younger brother?"

Archie looked across at her through the purple glow. "He fell onto some sharp rocks one hundred fifty feet below. He should have been dead, but he also possessed a special gift . . ."

The younger brother's mangled body began to reconstruct itself, his eyes growing round with amazement as his body was covered with a wicked-looking, powerful, black-scaled armor.

"The brothers swore that they would never be helpless again, but they ended up becoming just like the bullies. They used their newfound powers without any thought for the welfare of others. As they grew in power, they scoured the earth, looking for young people with superpowers who could be used for evil. They trained them to be supervillains like themselves and financed the whole operation by robbing banks."

Summer watched the orb as a wall exploded and several costumed villains entered through the rubble to rob a bank. A super-strong brute with iron arms ripped the vault door from a safe. A skinny villain dressed in purple slithered snake-like over to the frightened bank customers. His elongated face bore terrible fangs and scared a little boy who was huddled in the corner. Summer found herself watching and hoping that someone would stop them. A strange caped villain with a glowing globe for a head shouted to the others and gestured outside.

Suddenly rocketing through the window like a cannonball was Principal Zoom. The alien gritted his teeth and raised a strange-looking ray gun. Shingles exploded with a crash as another hero arrived on the scene. Summer could tell without thinking twice that the newest arrival was Captain Truehart. The father and son resemblance was uncanny.

"If it hadn't been for Principal Zoom and Captain Truehart, the villains would have taken over the world."

Summer watched as Zoom fired fizzing laser beams and strange ropelike strands from his space gun, immobilizing the villains in an otherworldly ooze. Truehart pummeled the others and soon they were forced to retreat.

Thunderclap continued.

"It is said that about thirteen years ago there was a fight between the two brothers and that one of them disappeared. The head of the school is now the older brother, Hieronimus Graves. Through some mysterious fluke, Graves recently discovered Captain Truehart's secret weakness."

Summer watched as Graves soared across the sky, his razor-sharp bat wings making him look like a flying demon. He clutched a small iron chest, and was flanked by flying troops of purple-and-ebony-clad villain students.

Captain Truehart, flashing through the cloudless sky like a golden bolt of lightning, rocketed skyward to meet the villains in midair. Summer watched as the young villains distracted him while Graves opened the chest. A small glittering jewel glowed from the chest's interior. Beams of purple light shot out of the jewel and coiled themselves like chains around the captain's chest. Truehart paused midair, stunned. His eyes widened with shock as his ability to fly disappeared.

As the captain plummeted to the ground, he made a desperate grab for Graves's leg and dragged him to the ground with him. The earth shattered under the impact of their fall.

Thunderclap and Summer watched soberly as the orb reduced in size and faded back into the Holotron. Thunderclap closed the lid.

"That last part happened six months ago. Hieronimus escaped, barely alive, back to his secret undersea lair. Everyone thought that he was gone for good. Yesterday, we received word that he has been seen again, and that he has recruited even more students. Most think that he wants to destroy the next generation of Zoom's students now that the captain is out of the way."

Summer shivered. Everything she saw in the orb was so disturbing. She felt like Graves could pop up at any moment and destroy the whole academy. How could she sleep tonight?

Thunderclap stared at the floor for a moment, deep in thought. "Somebody helped Graves obtain Captain Truehart's weakness from the weakness vault. The biggest mystery is . . . who?"

Thunderclap and Summer stood up. Thunderclap put the machine in his pocket.

Suddenly a thought occurred to Summer. "What happened to the younger brother?"

Thunderclap shrugged. "He just disappeared."

With a backward glance to make sure that they weren't being overheard, he lowered his voice. "Listen, tomorrow you are going to be tested. When they test you for your superpower, they will also discover your weakness. They will store a sample of it in a huge vault under the school. They keep it there in case of an emergency, like what happened at the mall earlier. Make sure you don't tell anybody what yours is. We don't know if there is a spy here at the school."

Summer nodded, and they both descended the ladders and went back to their rooms.

That night Summer lay awake a long time thinking about everything that she had seen. The image of Captain Truehart falling from the sky, his hand firmly gripping Graves's ankle as they tumbled miles through the air to the earth below, was burned into her memory.

She thought about Tommy. No wonder he acted the way he did. Summer felt sorry for him. She vowed that the next time she saw him, she would apologize for what had happened at Foggleberry's. With that thought, she finally fell asleep.

...10
THE TEST

SUMMER awoke to the sound of a ticking clock. She reached over to her nightstand, her mind already trying to think up another excuse not to go to school.

Her fingers probed for the snooze button on her *Gothic Girl* alarm clock. "Dad, I'm not going to go, I'm feeling . . . EEEEEEEEEEEK!"

Summer's fingers had not found her clock. Instead, she felt the tin-mustached face of a Zoom's robot.

"WHAT ARE YOU DOING IN MY ROOM?!" she shouted.

The robot stood expressionless, but its metal gears whirred anxiously. "*Bzzt. Click.* I'm sorry, Miss Jones. I am Zoom's Academy Regular Number 399. I have been sent to bring you to the testing facility."

"At least you could have knocked!" As she put on her glasses, the robot walked across her room and went outside, shutting the door behind him.

"Oh, boy, here we go." Summer rolled her eyes to the ceiling, anticipating the knock that came a couple of seconds later.

She called for the robot to come in. He did, obediently shutting the door behind him and resuming his place beside Summer's bed.

"Okay, okay, I didn't mean that you had to go back and do that. How much time do I have before the testing begins?"

"If you will excuse me, miss, the testing was supposed to begin forty-five minutes ago."

Great. Late already. Summer went into the bathroom to change her clothes.

"Do you have a name, or just a number?" she called from behind the door.

"*Bzzt.* If you wish, you may call me Clocksprocket."

Summer emerged from the bathroom wearing a Zoom's T-shirt and jeans. She just couldn't bring herself to wear the bright orange spandex suit that her dad had made for her.

"Do you think there would be any chance of getting some breakfast before we go? I'm starving!"

Clocksprocket's mustache twiddled merrily. "Of course, miss. I am equipped to provide self-contained culinary tasks. What do you wish to order?"

Summer thought.

"Well, how about a donut and a cup of hot chocolate?"

She had no sooner said it than Clocksprocket's gears began whirring and clicking noisily. He opened a side compartment and a cup fell into a holder. His fingertip swiveled back to reveal a small spout, which he placed over the cup. Hot cocoa poured from the nozzle into the cup. There was a small *ding* like an egg timer going off, and Clocksprocket opened the top of his head and removed a freshly made donut. He handed Summer her breakfast.

Summer looked at the items curiously for a moment, then tried a bite of the donut and a sip of cocoa.

"Wow. This is delicious! Thank you!"

Clocksprocket's mustache twiddled happily again. The two left the dormitory tree and set off for the testing center.

Clocksprocket walked with a mechanical gait that reminded Summer of a wind-up toy. He was fun to talk to. She found out that his incept date (or birthday) was fairly recent and that he was still new to the Zoom's campus.

"Were you one of the robots that greeted my dad and me when we landed yesterday?"

"*Whirr, click*. No, that was the Elite Guard."

Summer could have sworn that if it was possible for a robot to sigh, Clocksprocket had just done so.

"What's the matter?" asked Summer.

Clocksprocket was silent. Summer could hear his gears whirring and clicking away intensely, as if considering how to respond.

"I wish to join their number. I was informed yesterday that I must accomplish a great and heroic deed before I can be considered. I am hoping that an opportunity to do such a thing will present itself soon."

Summer had never imagined that a robot could have wants or desires. The movies usually made them seem as if they were only machines.

"Well, you seem like a good candidate to me. I'm sure you will get a chance to do something."

Clocksprocket continued to clump along in his jerky, mechanical way.

"It may be as you say, miss. *Whirr, click*. But my chances are slim. There have been no new additions to the Elite since the War of the Cryogenic Crusaders on Planet Ziff. When the guard was recruited to come to Zoom's, we other robots, the Regulars, were created to serve in a menial capacity. Unless something unexpected happens, my chances are precisely four hundred thousand ninety-two to one that I will ever be engaged in a situation to prove myself anything other than what I was created to be."

They rounded the walkway that led to the testing center. It was a squat, octagonal building covered with alternating mirrors and windows. Before Summer could think of anything encouraging to say to the robot, they had arrived in the reception area.

Clocksprocket handed Summer a small brass card with holes punched through it.

"Should you need anything, miss, simply place the card into any of the transmitting stations here on campus. I have been assigned specifically to meet your needs. Good day, miss."

Summer took the card and waved as Clocksprocket walked back outside, his big brass feet echoing off of the stainless-steel floor on his way out. Summer decided that she would use the card later. Maybe she could figure out a heroic task for the robot to do.

Two titanium doors covered in rivets swung open. Summer's dad and a bulging muscular man in a red and green costume walked over to greet her.

"Morning! You finally made it!"

Jasper strode over to Summer and gave her a quick hug.

"This is Dynamo. He will be giving you your first test."

Summer shook the immense man's hand.

"You don't have much time, so you better get started. I will catch up to you after the tests," Jasper said as he patted Summer good-bye.

At the mention of the word "test," Summer's stomach gave a lurch. She gazed up at the big man towering above her. She knew already that this was going to be embarrassing. She could barely lift her bicycle without getting a hernia! *Oh, well,* she thought, *I'll just go along with it. Who knows, maybe they can tap into some undiscovered reservoir of "supertalent" in me somewhere.*

She certainly didn't feel any different from the way she felt on any other morning in her life.

Dynamo led her through a laboratory filled with bubbling test tubes to a doorway that led to a large circular room. When they entered, Summer noticed a 1942 green Plymouth station wagon sitting in the middle of the floor.

"This is your first test." The man's booming voice echoed off of the walls. "I will be testing your strength aptitude. Don't be nervous. Every student who has ever passed the 'Ring Test' has registered a superpower. We are here to help you discover what yours might be."

He gave Summer a wink. She thought that even his eyelids must have muscles.

"Now then, I will demonstrate how this works. This car is hooked up to a sensor that will measure how much strength potential you possess. Even if you can't do this . . ."

Dynamo walked over to the car, and with a small grunt lifted it over his head with one hand. He paused for dramatic effect, then lowered the car back to the floor. Summer noticed that he was barely breathing hard.

"Any lifting movement is helpful. Even students with powers who are gifted in other areas can generally lift the wheels off of the ground a little."

He grabbed a clipboard, and put on a pair of reading glasses.

"Okay, let's begin. Please take a position by the car."

Summer did as she was told, and with her heart beating as if it would explode right out of her chest, she positioned herself by the back bumper, next to the license plate.

Dynamo fiddled with some knobs and checked a nearby monitor. He jotted down something in his notebook. Summer was pulling up on the bumper as hard as she could. She could see through the rear window to the opposite side where Dynamo stood. He appeared to be waiting for something. Summer lifted and strained. She poured every ounce of energy she had into lifting the car. Dynamo checked the monitor and wrote something down. She could feel the blood rushing into her face, and little flashing lights were beginning to dance in front of her eyes.

When would he tell her to stop? She felt as if she couldn't go on much longer. Was it her imagination, or had the car actually moved a little? She reached deep and redoubled her efforts. She was sure something had to be registering on the monitor!

Finally, he spoke.

"Okay, Summer, feel free to begin when ready."

Summer replied through gritted teeth, "I . . . AL . . . READY . . . START . . . ED . . ."

Dynamo turned to the monitor. He tapped the screen with a finger. "Is this thing on?"

Summer released the bumper with a gasp and fell backward onto the floor.

Dynamo grimaced and told Summer to go to the next testing station. Feeling weak and rather stupid, Summer followed the winding passageway down to Testing Station 2. She stepped through a pair of double doors and found herself in an incredible room.

Stars dotted the sky. A campfire glowed in a wooded thicket next to a small colorful gypsy wagon. Seated on the steps to the wagon was a woman wearing a beautiful silk dress and delicate gold jewelry.

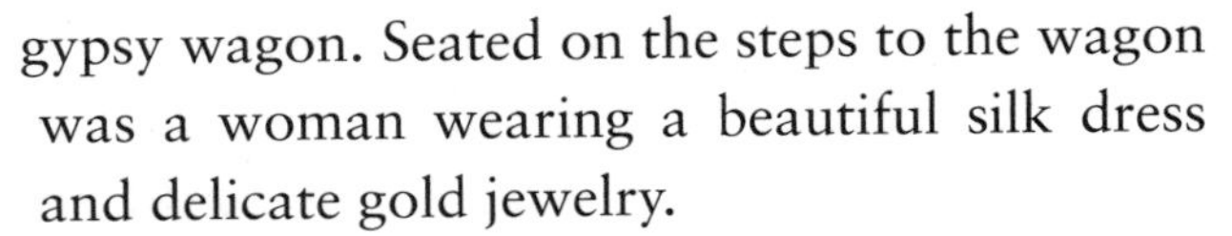

"Hello, you are Summer, no? You look a leetle bit like your father." She held up two fingers in a small pinching gesture to indicate the resemblance.

The woman's voice was thickly accented, as if she came from an Eastern European country.

"My name is Miss Zargovich, and I vill be testink you to find out if you have any powers of precognition."

When Summer looked confused, she replied, "Mind reading . . . Telepathy, if you prefer."

Summer followed her into the wagon, where a table was set up with several white cards on it. With a gentle sweeping gesture she removed the cards from the table and asked Summer to sit down.

"Now, here is vhat ve shall do." Miss Zargovich handed Summer a notepad and a pencil.

"I have several cards with different pictures on them. These you vill not look at vith your eyes, but you vill try to see vith your mind."

"Do I get a hint or anything?" asked Summer.

Miss Zargovich snorted delicately.

"No, no, silly girl. *Concentrate!* See the picture vith your mind. Visualize the picture on the card . . . Focus."

Summer took up the pencil and pad of paper. She didn't feel any impression coming to her at all. After a few excruciatingly long minutes Miss Zargovich checked the ancient-looking clock on her wall.

"Time's up. What did you come up with?"

Summer, with an embarrassed shrug, turned her pad over to reveal a childlike drawing of a house with smoke coming out of the chimney.

"Was I close?"

Miss Zargovich turned over her cards to reveal a series of numbers ranging from one to nine.

"No." She sighed. "Perhaps mental abilities is not for you, yes? You may move on to the next testink station I think . . ."

Summer smiled weakly and placed the writing utensil on the table and exited the wagon as gracefully as she could.

"This is ridiculous," she muttered. "I don't have any superpowers. I'm going to bomb out at this just like everything else I've tried to do in my life."

She walked down the twisting hallway, following the arrows outside the building to the next testing station. It was a huge stadium. It was ringed with gold and had a giant silver wing etched over the entrance. When Summer arrived inside she was greeted by a man wearing a winged cap and red tights. An emblem of a winged foot decorated his chest.

"Well,well,well,whathavewehere?SummerJones!Andalittlebitlate . . . five-pointtwosecondstobeexact. Nomatter!Gladyoumadeit!"

Summer was stunned by how fast the man could talk.

"Um . . . what?" Summer was so busy watching his lips move at blinding speed that she hardly heard what he said.

"Hey, Summer!" Thunderclap's familiar voice floated over to her from the stadium track.

Summer grinned and waved.

"This is my running coach, Mr. Fleet." Thunderclap indicated the fast-talking man. Summer noticed that Thunderclap was wearing a towel around his neck.

"What are you doing here?"

"Oh, I just finished setting a new record for the mile, and Mr. Fleet said I could hang out and watch you get tested."

She noticed that a floating screen hovered above the track and displayed Thunderclap's new record time; 32.5 seconds in glowing blue letters.

Mr. Fleet smiled at Summer. "ThunderclapiscurrentlyyourfasteststudenthereatZoom's. Hespeaksveryhighlyofyou. I'msurewecanexpectreallygreatthingsfromthedaughterofJasper-Jones. Shallwebeginthetesting?"

As they walked over to the starting blocks at the track, Summer moved close to Thunderclap.

"I don't know what you told him, but I don't think I've been doing very well with the tests today," she whispered.

Archie gave her shoulder an encouraging squeeze.

"Hey, that's all the more reason that you might be great at this one. All you have to do is think of really fast thoughts, you know? Like speeding bullets, airplanes, stuff like that."

Summer thought about her Phys. Ed. class at Jefferson. She remembered taking the Presidential Physical Fitness tests. It had been a living nightmare. She was laughed at for her abysmal time in running the fifty-yard dash.

"Runaroundthetrackfourtimesandcrossthefinishlineoverthere. Don'tworryifyouhapen-tobreakthesoundbarrier.Theacousticsinthestadiumcanhandleit."

"Break the sound barrier? Are you kidding?" Summer shielded her eyes from the sun and looked over toward the finish line.

"I can't even run around the block without getting a cramp in my side," she mumbled gloomily. "Oh, well, what the heck. Maybe my feet will start glowing or something and I'll be faster than a speeding bullet."

She mechanically began doing some stretching exercises she had learned in soccer practice.

"Maybe I just need to have a more positive attitude." She steeled her nerves. "Okay, Summer, you can do this . . . you're strong, you're fast, and you're going to amaze everyone! Including yourself!"

She repeated these thoughts in her mind as she moved to the starting blocks.

"Onyourmark . . ." Mr. Fleet raised a ray gun pistol into the air. "Getset . . ." Summer focused her eyes into the distance. She was concentrating on every fast-moving thing she could think of.

"GO!"

Summer leaped from the blocks. She could hear Thunderclap yelling for her, cheering her on.

It was much later, three hours and twenty-five minutes to be exact, that Summer finally crossed the finish line. She was wheezing and clutching her side. Mr. Fleet was gently snoring on one of the bleacher seats when she finally made it to the end. At one point Thunderclap had run up alongside of her, pacing her easily, and informed her that he was sorry but he couldn't stay and watch any longer, that he had to go help one of the teachers with running an errand.

"So much for thinking 'really fast thoughts,' " she muttered.

After catching her breath, she decided to leave the stadium quietly, not feeling it necessary to awake her snoring instructor.

The rest of the tests went pretty much the same.

In the Flying test, which was held at the top of one of the Sof' City skyscrapers, she managed to plummet fifty stories to the spongy street below. In the Communication with Water Animals evaluation, she was too embarrassed to put on a swimsuit so she didn't even take the test. In Elongation, the ability to stretch and shape-change, she stretched her arms out, straining to the point where she felt as if they would pop out of their sockets! Needless to say, she didn't show any aptitude in that one either.

Feeling exhausted and humiliated, Summer met up with her dad at the end of the day. Jasper puffed on his pipe thoughtfully.

"Honey, I don't know what the problem is. Everybody who has tested with the ring has a power of some kind. We just have to discover what yours is. I will be meeting with the faculty tonight to discuss everything. Don't worry."

... 11
NEW FRIENDS

SUMMER *was* worried, however. After her dad said good night outside of the dorm tree, she was relieved to find Thunderclap waiting for her at her room.

"I don't know what is wrong with me." Summer sat cross-legged on the floor of the futuristic-looking cottage. Thunderclap sat down in a floating hammock.

"What are you talking about?"

"Well, it's just this. Back home in California, I hated Jefferson Junior High more than anything. It was awful there. I could never fit in."

Thunderclap was reclining on the hammock and propped himself up on an elbow to listen.

"I'm just afraid that I'll blow it here and get sent back. I don't seem to be able to fit in anywhere I go. I'm not good at anything I try to do. Am I destined to be a loser or what?"

Thunderclap looked at her thoughtfully. "Well," he said, "you seem like a cool person to me. You should have seen me when I first discovered my superpowers!"

Summer looked up. "What happened?"

"There I was, riding my bike in the rain." Thunderclap waved his hands dramatically. "I was late for band practice at school, and decided to take a shortcut across a golf course. Bad idea! I had my trumpet in one hand and was trying to practice the *William Tell Overture* when a bolt of lightning came from nowhere, struck the trumpet, and knocked me fifty feet into the air!"

Summer goggled at Thunderclap. "I was amazed that it didn't kill me! So after a minute or so, I got up and got back on my smoking bike. I wanted to hightail it outta there; I didn't want to take any chances, y'know? So I started pedaling as fast as I could. But it suddenly felt like someone had strapped me to a Porsche or something! I was so fast that before I knew it, I was off of the golf course and had pedaled through a window and into the mall across the street!" Thunderclap chuckled and shook his head. "You shoulda seen me. Man, it was pathetic. I was screaming like a little girl, ricocheting off of the escalator and into the walls like I was a pinball in some giant, life-sized pinball machine." Summer grinned. "I was so scared that when I finally did make it home, I locked myself in my room and wouldn't come out. Thankfully I have really cool parents. After calming me down, they knew to call Zoom's and a couple of days later two guys in superhero costumes showed up at our house to give me the 'Ring Test.' Man, it's a good thing they showed up! I still wouldn't know what I was doing if it hadn't been for them."

"You're lucky to have cool parents." Summer picked at the sole of her tennis shoe distractedly. "Mine divorced when I was six. I guess it seems like a lot of stuff started going wrong for me at that point."

Thunderclap started to interrupt, but Summer held out a placating hand.

"Oh, my dad is okay, I guess."

Thunderclap nodded in agreement.

She continued. "It's just that he is so weird! It's like, I know he loves me, but he's always making these stupid inventions that hardly ever work and . . . and he and my mom never really told me why they divorced . . . I dunno. It's stupid I guess. But I just kinda felt like maybe it was my fault."

Summer gazed down at the floor self-consciously. There was an awkward pause.

"Hey, maybe you are just worrying about things way too much. You wouldn't be here if you didn't pass the 'Ring Test.' It did glow blue, right?"

She was grateful for the change of subject.

"Right."

"Well then, I bet it's just because you have some really special ability that nobody has ever even seen yet! You could be, like, the next 'Ultra Woman' or something!"

Thunderclap sat up on the hammock.

"Besides, it's going to be different for you here at Zoom's. Trust me. This is a really cool place. Tomorrow we get to start our classes. We train during the day at our 'Equipping Stations,' then at night we get to go to Megapolis with an instructor and fight actual supervillains! It really beats sitting in some stuffy classroom all day."

They were interrupted by a knock on the door.

Thunderclap grinned. "That must be the guys. I invited some friends over for you to meet."

Summer was greeted by a rather odd assortment of boys who were her own age. The first, a mammoth boy named Kibosh, was dressed in a crimson and blue suit and wore a space helmet. The next, a stretchy, noodlelike guy in purple and gray with a tousled mop of blond hair, was Earthworm. The third, fat and tiny, flew around their heads with insect wings and was named Beetlebomb.

Summer shyly shook their friendly outstretched hands. The last boy she met, and certainly the most odd-looking, was a kid known only as "Birthday Boy." Summer couldn't help staring at him. His face had a blue-gray pallor, and he had deep black circles around his eyes as if he had never slept a day in his life. He wore a pointed black-and-white-striped birthday hat, and when he said "*Hello*" it was in a cold voice that sent shivers down her spine.

"Guys, this is Summer Jones."

"Hey, is she any relation to Moon Man?" Beetlebomb's voice squeaked above Summer's head.

Thunderclap turned to Summer. "That's your dad's hero name."

He swatted at Beetlebomb, who easily dodged his friendly jab. "Yeah, she's Mr. Jones's daughter."

"Hey, we don't care what they say, we like your dad." Kibosh's deep voice boomed.

"Yes. He is very . . . interesting . . . one of the few teachers who actually challenge the mind." The gray-faced Birthday Boy said this with a resigned air and a smug expression. He enunciated each word carefully, as if English were a difficult language for him to speak.

"BB here is from another dimension." Thunderclap indicated him with a nod. "He is at Zoom's because of some kind of interdimensional space and time error. Tell her, B. . . ."

"Well, to put it into terms that you terrestrial dwellers would understand . . . It was my birthday, my twelfth to be precise." Birthday Boy had a faraway look in his shadowed eyes. "Birthdays are celebrated pretty much the same in every dimension. I had a cake, candles, and the usual trimmings. It would have been like any other, except for the fact that when it came time for me to make a wish, I did something, well, that should never have been done in my quadrant of the universe." At this he paused and shifted uncomfortably. "I made my wish . . . I wished that it could be my birthday every day. The result was catastrophic." He grimaced.

"A birthday wish can be something very

powerful, and my wish changed the fabric of space and time forever. The wish was granted, you see, and it meant that in order for me to have my birthday every day somebody, somewhere, was never born. You can see how that might complicate things . . ."

Summer had never really thought about the repercussions of such a wish. She thought about what kind of place Earth might be without the great people who made significant changes to our past or present. What would have happened without them?

Birthday Boy continued. "I was visited by a man named Candlewick, well, not really a man. He would look more to you like a talking candle. Anyway, to make a long story short, I must spend my lifetime at age twelve jumping throughout time and space, trying to take the place of the person who was never born and keep reality what it is supposed to be."

He shrugged as if this were as common as saying, "I spilled a glass of milk and had to clean it up." Thunderclap nodded seriously.

"He's at Zoom's because sometime in a past that we know nothing about there was a hero kid who grew up to be somebody named 'Colossal Man' who was never born. Supposedly, he saved the world at some point."

"Do you have any superpowers?" asked Summer. Birthday Boy looked away and got very quiet.

Beetlebomb squeakily interrupted the awkward moment. "He does, but we don't talk about them much. They're really *creepy.*" The little bug boy shuddered before continuing, changing the subject. "My powers are that I can blow up! Wanna see?"

At that point Kibosh, Earthworm, and Thunderclap all began shouting "NO!" at the same time.

Summer couldn't help giggling at Beetlebomb's eager expression. "What do you mean 'blow up'?"

Beetlebomb, looking affronted, continued. "I can explode at will . . . yes . . . a little messy sometimes," he admitted, "but I'm kind of like a grenade going off. The great part is that I can put myself together again." He beamed proudly.

Earthworm snaked out a long arm and flicked him across the room. They all laughed as he bounced off of a lamp and into Summer's laundry basket.

"Have you been tested to find out what your superpower is yet, Summer?" Kibosh asked as he smiled at her.

Summer was awkwardly fumbling for an answer.

Thunderclap spoke up, seeing Summer's distress. "Sorry, man, it's top secret. She's got something so new and powerful it's not even on the books!"

Summer blushed and smiled at him gratefully.

Kibosh looked impressed. "I think that's great, because we are going to need all the help we can get tomorrow night. I heard that the students at Graves are going to try to rob the Megapolis Museum of Modern Art."

Beetlebomb's muffled voice came from the laundry. "Yeah, dangerous stuff. They probably want to steal 'Brown's Requiem.' I heard that it is worth a fortune!"

Beetlebomb emerged with a sock on his tiny head. "The museum is rigged with all kinds of laser beams and motion detectors to protect it. I heard that that one painting is worth more than the contents of fifty banks!"

Summer felt more than a little nervous at the prospect of going down into a city filled with dangerous criminals.

Thunderclap saw her panicky expression and reassured her. "Relax, you'll have an instructor with you, remember?" he whispered and winked.

Clocksprocket's voice echoed from behind Summer's door. "*Bzzt. Click*. May I enter, miss?"

Summer called for him to come in.

"Hey, cool! Snacks!" Beetlebomb licked his lips hungrily and flew over to Clocksprocket, who had entered holding a giant tray loaded with freshly baked chocolate chip cookies.

Thunderclap's eyes widened, impressed. "Whoa, Summer. You didn't tell me that you had a Regular! Man, those things are really expensive."

Summer grinned. She was feeling really good, much better than she had felt only a couple of hours earlier. Who knew? Maybe Thunderclap was right, maybe she did have some kind of secret ability that the school had never seen. She joined in with her new friends and munched happily, feeling optimistic for the first time in ages.

...12 JASPER'S SECRET

IN a blue room lit by the glow of an atomic accelerator, the faculty of Zoom's Academy met to discuss the outcome of Summer Jones's test. Principal Zoom, now wearing a suit of sparkling, scaly material, led the meeting.

"Ladies and gentlemen . . ."

His goggled eyes scanned the various faculty members sitting behind the large floating table.

"I have read the test results for Miss Jones, but find the results a bit unusual and disturbing. Mr. Fleet, will you begin by relating exactly what happened during your test?"

Mr. Fleet stood up. The assembled faculty, about fifty men and women in heroic costumes, turned to listen.

"YesProfessor. Thisiskindofawkward . . ."

Principal Zoom held up his hand. "Forgive me, Thaddeus, but would you mind if I turn on the vocal manipulation translator? My alien ears, I'm afraid, are not what they used to be." Principal Zoom pushed a small button on a console. Mr. Fleet continued with his voice slowed down to a normal cadence.

"No problem, Professor. As I was saying, this is a little awkward. I feel I should start by apologizing to Jasper."

Jasper was sitting at the far end of the table, and acknowledged Fleet's apology with a small nod.

"My tests, unfortunately, showed that Summer Jones has no heroic abilities at all. In fact, I checked the Cosmic Odometers at the track several times for even the slightest registration. They indicated that the results were low for even nonheroic standards." He turned toward Jasper with a look of compassion on his face. "That isn't to say she isn't a nice kid and all, Jasp, but . . ." He shrugged.

Dynamo and Miss Zargovich stood up. Dynamo lifted his chin and boomed, "My findings were the same. She couldn't budge the car an inch. I've seen infants with heroic powers able to at least do that."

Miss Zargovich interrupted him. "I must agree with my husband. The child is completely mortal. She does not belong at the school."

The teachers began to murmur. Jasper stood up and placed his hands on the table.

"Now wait a minute! She passed the Ring Test. I saw it with my own eyes. The Academy Constitution clearly states that the word of a faculty member on this matter is binding." He glared around the room defiantly. "Maybe she has a power that we don't have on record yet!"

The commotion increased. A pretty lady in pink tights and white cape stood up.

"Jasper is right," she said. "However improbable, there might be some power that we haven't discovered yet." She smiled at Jasper. "Surely Jasper's impeccable record as a faculty member demands that we give her an opportunity to prove herself."

Jasper smiled back at the woman with his ears reddening slightly.

"Miss Avian, I do not doubt that you, of all people, would support Jasper Jones . . . this 'Moon Man' as he calls himself."

The speaker emerged from the center of the table, rising through the surface like a holographic projection. He was small, but his presence exuded an unearthly strength.

"I, for one, believe that there might be a different reason that the child has not exhibited any heroic powers. I believe we are forgetting a very important detail, one that Mr. Jones might not want us to call again to memory."

At this statement the room fell into a hushed, tense silence. All eyes were on Jasper, who looked a little nervous, but glared at the speaker defiantly.

"Let us not forget that Jasper Jones once embodied all that we have fought against, that his brother is currently the head of the organization we most despise. I say, once a villain . . . ALWAYS A VILLAIN!" The figure spat out the last part of his sentence like it was venom.

Angry shouts filled the room, most defending Jasper and angry at the small, cloaked figure's accusation. Principal Zoom called for silence.

"Mysterion, I understand your reticence at accepting Jasper as one of our own. You have made your position clear from the very moment that he left Graves and came to us. But let me be perfectly clear . . ."

At this the diminutive professor seemed to grow in size. His voice was level, but rang with authority.

"I am the principal of this noble institution and the ultimate decision of who is elected to the faculty rests with me. I do not regret my decision to allow Jasper to be a part of our school, nor will I allow the topic of his past involvement with the enemy to be discussed again." He looked pointedly at Mysterion, who glared back mutely.

Zoom pointed his three-fingered hand around the room, indicating the entire faculty.

"I don't want a word of this matter mentioned outside of this room, especially not to Summer Jones." His voice softened. "I am inclined to agree with Jasper's and Miss Avian's assessment. Let's allow for some time on this matter. Miss Jones will attend classes at this school and be treated like any other student. Perhaps her powers will manifest themselves in a way none of us can expect or understand. This meeting is adjourned."

As the teachers filed out, discussing the situation in low voices, Miss Avian and Fleet walked over to Jasper.

Fleet slapped Jasper on the back good-naturedly. "Don't worry about a thing, Jasp, she's a great kid. Everything will be fine."

Jasper looked a little shaken up from the meeting, but managed a small smile.

Miss Avian hugged him. "Aw, Jasp, you should have seen her over at Sof' City. Poor thing." She looked at Jasper, her eyes filled with compassion. "She was completely terrified of being at the top of one of the buildings, but was really determined to try and prove that she had some powers. When she fell . . . well, even though the streets are soft as a pillow, I couldn't help flying down to catch her."

"Thanks, Betty. I don't know . . ." Jasper ran his hand through his hair in frustration. "I know what I saw. The ring wouldn't have glowed blue if she didn't have some kind of heroic power." He gazed up at the ceiling. "She's had to go through so much, ever since the divorce and everything."

Miss Avian smiled at Jasper reassuringly. "Cheer up. It's gonna work out fine, okay?"

She put her arm around him as they walked out of the council room. "You want to grab a latte at Creampuff's?"

Jasper chuckled and looked down at Miss Avian. He gave her a half hug and winked. "Sounds good."

...13 THE EQUIPPING STATIONS

THE next day dawned blue, bright, and clear. Summer greeted her first day of classes with uncharacteristic anticipation. She even decided to wear the superhero costume that her dad had made for her, ignoring the less-than-tasteful color scheme.

I'll just go with it for now, she told herself. *Maybe I can get something a little more fashionable later.*

After all, it seemed like just about everyone had a costume of some kind on the campus. She decided that at some point she would sit down with a pencil and paper and try to sketch something closer to her liking.

She glanced down at her schedule as she paced down the hallway.

"Let's see, 'Super-Vehicle Operation' at Equipping Station 7. This should be interesting."

She had spent a late night with her new friends, and was surprised at how differently she felt about Zoom's. Sure, her friends were a little quirky, but having friends was something new for Summer and she found that it made a huge difference in how she felt about going to school.

As she walked to her first class she suddenly heard a quiet voice behind her that made her stop in her tracks.

"Your name is Summer Jones, right?"

It was Tommy Truehart. He wore a bandage around his wrist, but otherwise looked the same as when she had seen him at Foggleberry's. The most noticeable difference this time, however, was that he was smiling.

"Yeah. That's me."

She fidgeted nervously, pushing her glasses back on her nose self-consciously.

Tommy walked closer. "Hey, no hard feelings about yesterday . . . okay? I guess I went a little crazy in there. I hope you weren't hurt or anything?"

Summer found herself hypnotized by the handsome boy's change in demeanor. He had seemed like a bit of a bully yesterday, but now . . . Summer found her palms starting to sweat and she blushed furiously. "No, were you? I'm really sorry about what happened, I don't really know myself, but I'm glad to see that you look okay. Great actually."

Her face turned an even brighter shade of pink. She couldn't believe she had just said that!

Tommy laughed. "The nurse patched me up, thankfully I heal fast."

They began walking back down the hall together. "I don't do too well with crowds. It kinda freaks me out when people start talking about my dad."

Summer felt a wave of sympathy for Tommy. "I heard what happened. I'm sorry."

Tommy looked down. "Thanks. My dad was pretty special around here. He was really unique."

"Well, I can relate a little bit to what it's like to have a dad who's kind of different."

"Yeah, your dad is Mr. Jones, the, uh, 'Moon Man,' right?"

Summer nodded. They approached the door to Equipping Station 5 "Secret Identities."

"Well, this is my class. See you around." Tommy flashed her a grin and ducked into the classroom.

Summer's feet seemed to float off of the ground. She was standing in the hall, staring after Tommy, when she felt a tap on her shoulder.

"What in the heck were you talking to *him* for?" Thunderclap looked annoyed.

Summer answered Thunderclap with a dreamy expression on her face. "He was nice."

Summer could tell that Thunderclap thought that there was nothing "nice" about Tommy at all.

"Just be careful, that guy is trouble. I know it." They walked down the hallway to Summer's classroom.

"Hey, Super-Vehicle Operation! I wanted to add that class but it was full." Summer stood outside the door and peeked inside. A space age–looking car with a turbine engine sat revolving slowly and majestically on a platform. The excited chatter of the students filled the room as they took their seats.

"I'd better go. Do you want to meet later for lunch?"

Thunderclap nodded. "Sure, I'll save you a seat at Captain Creampuff's. Have fun!" Summer's instructor, Wombat, was a short, stocky man in a black and gold costume. "Awright, siddown. Let's get staahted."

His Aussie accent was a little muffled by the sharp-eared mask he wore. Summer took her seat and listened.

"I'm 'ere to teach you 'ow to operate a beautiful machine loik this one 'ere." He gestured at the sleek car. "When a hero doesn't 'ave a sidekick, his best friend is his auto." He removed a remote control from his utility belt and pressed a button.

Immediately the car transformed; its seemingly impenetrable surface broken by armored plates that slid away to reveal the door. The control panel inside was full of blinking lights and space-age techno gadgetry.

"Now, before we take 'er for a spin, who wants to be the first to sit inside for a demo?"

Hands shot up all over the room. Summer was as impressed as the rest of the class, but didn't raise her hand. The Wombat walked right over to her desk and said, "'Ow 'bout this Sheila 'ere? Come on up and 'ave a seat insoyde." Summer assumed that "Sheila" meant "girl" in Aussie-speak, and timidly followed him up to the car.

The seat was made of black leather that contoured perfectly to the driver's form. It felt wonderful! She imagined how envious the kids back home would be if they saw her drive up to school in this!

"Now then, Oy want you to press the green button ovah there." Wombat indicated a button on the far side of the console. Summer did as she was told, and the class "oohed and ahhed" appreciatively as the far wall of the classroom slid sideways to reveal a runway that led to a waiting test track.

"And that's just the garage openah! This baby has got everything you could evah want . . . smoke screen, oil slicks, missiles, even an eighteen-stack CD changah with a full surround sound speakah system!"

Most of the boys in the class stared at the car with pure unbridled adoration.

"Righteous!" said Wonder Frog, a short red-haired boy with big goggles and flipper feet.

"Now, Oy know that most of ya don't 'ave your licenses yet." Wombat held up his hand trying to silence the disappointing groans. "But this cah is equipped with an autopilot function that will self-correct any driving mistakes." The class brightened.

"One word of warning though. Whatevah you do, don't press the red button. It takes the cah out of auto and engages the turbine thrusters."

"Now then, 'ow about a test drive, eh?" Wombat smiled at Summer, showing a row of very sharp white teeth. Summer nodded, too excited to speak.

"Okay, now, just ease down gently on that pedal ovah there."

Summer did as she was told. The car began to rev up and the runway lights flashed in sync, pointing her way to the test track.

"You're doing great. Now, gently push that levah on your right side down." Summer reached for the lever.

As soon as the lever was released, the doors clicked and slammed back into place. She moved her hand back to the wheel, and accidentally brushed a small knob. There was a small whirring noise, then a CD started playing a pulse-pounding sound track. Wombat was gesturing outside of the window. Summer tried to hear him but couldn't because the music inside the car was too loud! She frantically searched for the knob that had turned on the CD player. There were buttons everywhere!

Then the unthinkable happened. She was reaching for what she thought might be the knob when her elbow accidentally punched the red button. There was a sound of thunder. Summer's heart sank.

Suddenly the car rocketed through the classroom and down the runway like a jet plane! Students dove from their desks just in time as the car blasted through the room. Summer couldn't tell which scream was louder, hers or the turbine engine's! She panicked, not having the slightest idea of how to stop, and cowered in the seat with her hands covering her eyes.

The wreck that followed would have made an action movie producer drool. The car smashed into the test track wall, jumped over the bleachers, hurtled fifty yards through the air, and landed, crashing into the side of the Administration Building with a terrific crunch made all the more spectacular by the mushroom-cloud ball of flame that followed. Students and faculty members were screaming and running away from the wreckage. If it hadn't been for the car's super-advanced safety features, most of the witnesses were convinced that nobody could have walked away alive from a wreck of that magnitude.

Summer was removed, shaking and coughing, from the crushed heap, and taken to the nurse's office to be checked out.

She was released shortly thereafter. Surprisingly, she had only suffered a tiny scratch on her forearm, and was told that she could finish her classes for the day. Wombat blamed himself for the accident, and assured Summer that it wasn't her fault. Summer appreciated the gesture, but knew the truth. She had really "messed up."

The rest of the day was filled with minor catastrophes in all of her classes. She dropped her next class, "X-Ray Vision," when she spotted a leering boy wearing a strange pair of glasses, chasing a group of screaming girls down the hallway. In Miss Powers's "Costume Design" class she managed to accidentally spill the contents of a utility belt's sleeping gas capsule and knocked out half of the class until the bell rang.

In Sof' City, the students were instructed to fire a grappling hook from their utility belts, swing to the street below, and tackle an inflatable "thug" who was poised at a bank robbery. One by one the students took a turn, sliding down their cables from high atop one of the Sof' skyscrapers. Most of the kids were having the time of their lives, bouncing on the recoiling surfaces of the streets as if they were on a huge trampoline.

When it was Summer's turn, she gazed down at the long drop below with sweaty apprehension. After five attempts, she finally got her grappling hook to stick, but the hook accidentally popped one of the school's new inflatable vehicles and she dropped her grappling gun. To make matters worse, the gun fell fifty floors and ended up hitting Stephanie Farnsworth, "Ruby Avenger," on the back of the head.

Feeling very discouraged and frustrated, she arrived at her dad's own class: "Utility Belt Engineering." She was dismayed to hear one of the students whispering nearby that most of them thought that her dad's class was a "joke" and that it didn't require any "real powers" at all. The bell rang and her dad entered the classroom. He looked a little frazzled, like he had been in a hurry, running late for class. He lit his pipe and took a roll count. Summer was doubly embarrassed when he decided to make a point of mentioning that she was his daughter in front of the whole class.

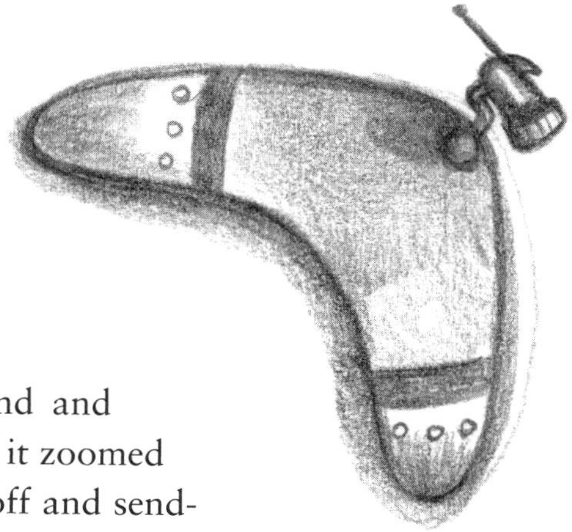

Jasper attempted to show the class his latest crime-fighting invention, the jet-powered boomerang. But when he started it up, it blasted out of his hand and bounced around the room with wild abandon. Finally, it zoomed back at the panicked Jasper's head, knocking his hat off and sending him crashing into the wastebasket. When the bell rang signaling the end of class, Summer overheard a few of the students from her previous classes whisper, "Like father like daughter," under their breath as they left through the door.

Summer met Thunderclap for lunch. When she sadly related the events of her terrible day he assured her that he would personally try to research what her particular superpower might be. Summer was comforted a little, but what she really wanted was for the whole day to end as soon as possible.

. . . 14 GRAVES ACADEMY

THE brass jaws of the hideous skulls that adorned the ancient pipe organ opened and closed, emitting the haunting notes of J. S. Bach's *Toccata and Fugue*. The organist, a pasty-faced, pug-nosed boy wearing a mask that was split in half, giggled insanely as the music swelled to its majestic, eerie crescendo.

"HAAA HAAA AAHHHHHHH!" His evil laughter echoed in the vaulted chamber. Several of the Graves Academy's students watched as he finished the piece.

"Bravo! Well done. Class, did you notice how his eyes bugged out at the end of the piece? Theatrics. To be a truly terrifying supervillain you must never underestimate the value of a maniacal expression. Very nice work, Ripsaw, you may rejoin the others." Ripsaw twisted his lips into a half sneer, and slid off of the organ bench.

"Mr. Fiend?"

The green-faced, ghoulish instructor turned to acknowledge the voice. It came from a sallow-skinned girl wearing a black ruffled party dress and a matching bow covered with skulls.

"Yes, Lucifina?"

"I was just wondering, is it okay to kill the hero while the music is still playing, or should one wait until the piece is finished?"

"An excellent question." The monstrous teacher smiled, baring his yellowed fangs. "This is an area that is largely left up to the individual. Speaking for myself, I always enjoy stretching out a hero's demise as long as possible."

The class murmured appreciatively.

He tapped a finger against his wart-covered chin. "Now, let's see. Who will be next?" His yellow cat eyes scanned the assembled students. "Ah, Blue Ox, please come forward."

A big blue boy with huge black horns growing out of his head approached the bench. It protested loudly as he placed his enormous posterior upon it. He cracked his knuckles loudly, paused with a dignified air, and then began to play.

A look of confusion appeared on the instructor's face. What was that behemoth playing? It sounded like the "Beer Barrel Polka."

"Stop! STOP!" Mr. Fiend roared at the boy, who stopped and looked up innocently. "What, may I ask, was that?" The boy stared back stupidly.

"A polka. I learned it from my ma back home in Minnesoooota." The boy's voice had a heavy midwestern accent.

Mr. Fiend rubbed his temples. "Blue," he growled, "the name of my class is Music for the Malevolent Mind. *Malevolent* mind! If you go through all of the trouble of setting up a death trap, the music must complement the occasion. Can you imagine how the hero would feel if he were suspended over a vat of boiling acid as a razor-sharp pendulum was slowly cutting away the thin rope that held his precious life and you were to launch into a song like THAT?"

The boy hung his head.

"He might laugh. Or, even worse, ask you for a bratwurst and a beer." He gave the boy a withering stare. "Go back and learn something more appropriate."

Blue Ox sloped from the bench, embarrassed, and rejoined his group of disdainful peers.

In a jagged cavelike room across the hall, other students practiced fighting techniques. The teacher, a darkly beautiful snake woman named Slithestra, watched as a boy wearing a black costume covered with a clock pattern punched and kicked a generic, hero-styled robot. The robot fired a ray gun at the boy, who dodged the sizzling beams.

"Don't forget, Overtime, use your sssssspeed to your advantage," she hissed. The boy shot into super speed, leaping over the laser beams, and landing a dozen punches in the blink of an eye.

The robot, unable to block the lightning-fast assault, crumpled to the ground, dropping its ray gun. Overtime stepped back as the robot raised itself to its knees and asked nicely to have its gun back. The boy nodded and waited while the robot reequipped itself before continuing the fight. Just as Overtime was about to punch, a long coiled arm shot out and cracked him upside his head.

"Owwww!" the boy yelped. "What did I do?" The beautiful woman's head stretched on an elongated neck to eye level.

"You never . . . never allow a hero a fighting chance. NEVER! We bite, we kick, and we pull hair. THERE ARE NO RULES!"

Down a smoky corridor, in a room that resembled a psychologist's office, several students sat taking copious notes. A tired-looking vampiric figure lectured in a droning voice about the importance of recovering from defeat.

"Nine times out of ten you will lose. That is just the way it is."

He held up a long-fingered hand. "Good prevails most of the time, don't ask me why it is," he muttered and sighed. "After three hundred years in this business I still do not know why."

He thrust his finger in the air for emphasis. "*But,* many a great villain has underestimated the power of persistence! You must never give up! The heroes never do, so we must not either! You must get up again. Look at me. I rise from the dead every morning."

He paced in front of the class, his ebony cape billowing out behind him. "Do I always feel like getting up? Are there times that Dr. Vlad would rather stay in his coffin?" He held out his hands in a placating gesture. "Of course. But I do not let it stop me."

Dr. Vlad's piercing stare scanned the room. "Evil never rests. We must work twice as hard as they do. It is part of the job."

In a laboratory classroom titled "Diabolical Death traps" several students worked feverishly at their torturous inventions. Their instructor, a man with metal crab pincers for hands, looked on proudly as ingenious traps sliced and diced hero dummies into shreds.

In an observation window high above the classroom, the horrific face of Hieronimus Graves watched with a proud and cruel smile. His glittering eyes gazed at his newest breed of villains, pleased with their progress. His hands traveled down to a console, and lifted an old-fashioned microphone from its cradle.

A hissing crackle, some feedback, then a sinister, booming voice echoed throughout the entire school. "Ladies and gentlemen . . ."

Everyone froze, listening attentively.

"I am pleased to announce that tonight's raid is proceeding as planned. May I remind you, failure to attend your assigned duty is not an option. Any student who wishes to be excused from the mission will be summarily executed. Very painfully, I might add. All students are to report to Crimson Claw and Purple Fang. They will be your supervising instructors for this evening's robbery. That is all. Death to Zoom's."

The cry was immediately echoed throughout the school, the phrase every student learned on arriving at the underwater fortress, the passionate desire of every supercriminal in the world. "Death to Zoom's!"

Graves marched back to his private chambers with the loyal cries of his minions echoing behind him. Once inside, he closed the heavy chamber doors for a private meeting with his most trusted faculty members.

"How is the mission planning proceeding?"

A heavyset man with the head of a bull terrier replied.

"All is gooood, master. The information has been leaked to Zoom's that we will be robbing the museum."

Graves sat down on an ornate throne, wincing slightly as he propped his leg gingerly upon a silk ottoman.

"Excellent, Phydeux. Begin Phase Two of the plan. I want all of their attention to be on the museum while we steal the Plasmatic Destabilizer from the Scientific Research Institute."

Phydeux snapped a quick salute and strode from the room. Graves turned his attention to a tiny figure that crouched near his throne. "And what of the girl?"

The wicked little figure, which resembled a Polynesian tiki god, moved its wooden jaws weakly for a moment, then a high-pitched, whistling voice emerged from its tiny throat.

"Your brother's daughter is at the school. They have not yet determined what her power is."

Graves smiled cruelly. "The fools. They pride themselves on their 'high-tech' testing devices and yet they can't even see the obvious." He chuckled.

"Once we have obtained the Destabilizer we can penetrate the force field that surrounds the weakness vault. Our agent has done well. Inform him that I will see to it that he is well rewarded for his efforts."

"But, Your Excellency"—the tiny god turned its blind eyes upon Graves—"will he not be spotted? There has been much attention drawn to him as of late."

Graves's eyes narrowed. "I will use my powers to rectify that situation. You will see, Kapu."

Graves leaned his head back upon his richly padded throne. "I will not be denied.

Now that Captain Truehart is gone, I will obtain the weaknesses and drive Principal Zoom to his knees. Then I shall acquaint myself with my dear niece. By the time we have harnessed her powers and taken over the world, the slow-witted faculty at Zoom's will only then realize what they have lost."

"But what if the girl will not comply?"

Graves shot the idol a withering look.

"Oh, she will. She will be made to understand that it is Fate that makes us who we are. She has no choice. It is her heritage. Her destiny."

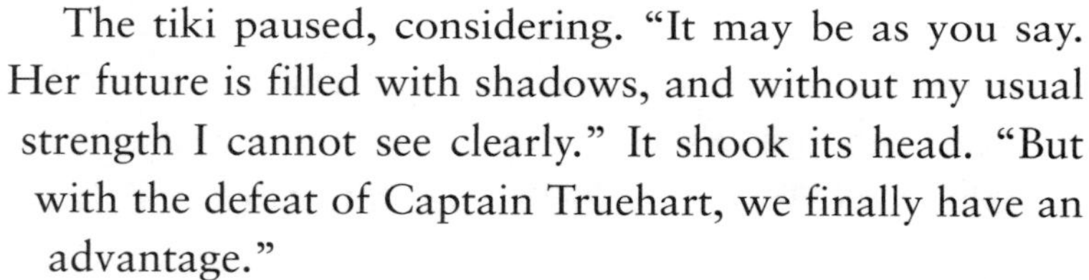

The tiki paused, considering. "It may be as you say. Her future is filled with shadows, and without my usual strength I cannot see clearly." It shook its head. "But with the defeat of Captain Truehart, we finally have an advantage."

The god clenched his oversized teeth together. "Oooooooh," he moaned. "You have given me so few sacrifices. I grow so hungry."

Graves looked down at the god fondly. "Don't worry, my friend. Soon that will change and you will be strong once again."

The tiki's eyes glowed red with pleasure. "Then I shall feast?"

"Oh, yes." Graves smiled down at the statue. "You will not be hungry again for a long time, I think . . ."

...15

THE LETTER

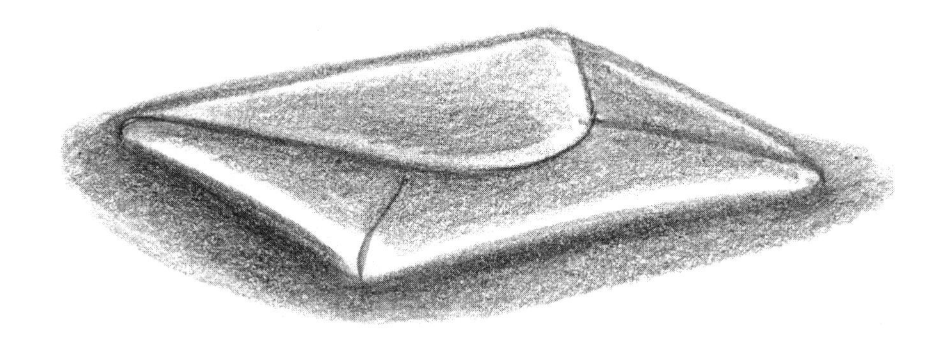

SUMMER sat with Jasper underneath a large oak tree. Her eyes were downcast as she rested her chin on her knees.

"I made you a special utility belt for your mission tonight."

Jasper smiled as he offered a belt with capsule compartments around its perimeter to Summer. "There is an electromagnetic net in that one." He pointed to the various capsules with his pipe stem. "And over here is a smoke screen." He looked pointedly at Summer.

"Until we discover what your power is you may need to use that one . . . Be careful, make yourself invisible to your enemy if you have to."

Summer didn't look up.

Jasper looked at her with a puzzled expression on his face, then he brightened. "Oh, I know what it is. You're having the 'first-mission' jitters."

He put a comforting hand on her shoulder and smiled. "Don't worry about it. Everything will be fine. I think Wombat is going with your group tonight. He's a real pro."

Summer shrugged her dad's hand off of her shoulder.

"Hey, what's the matter?" Jasper looked concerned.

"You wouldn't understand," Summer said reproachfully. "You brought me to this dumb place, building it up like it would be 'great' and all."

She glared at her dad. "And here I am, no superpowers. Nothing special about me at all. Zippo." Summer got up and paced restlessly.

"In case you haven't noticed, I'm not more powerful than any locomotives or leaping high buildings in a single bound. I'm not. I'm definitely not 'hero' material."

Her voice rose in anger.

"I'm just a stupid thirteen-year-old girl with an absentminded father who can't get anything right!" Tears were burning in her eyes. Jasper looked hurt. Summer stomped her foot and ran down the hill. She could hear her dad's voice calling after her, but she kept running and pretended not to listen.

She ran all the way to the other side of the campus before finally getting tired and deciding to go back to the tree house. When she arrived, the sun was going down. Feeling emotionally exhausted, she exited the elevator that went up the tree's trunk, and entered her dorm cottage.

On her bed was a note from her dad. He must have left it for her after she ran away from him. She opened it and read,

Dear Summer,

Being a hero isn't about how fast you can run, or how strong you are, or even about how you look in costume! It's about doing what is right no matter what the cost. It's about never giving up, even when you feel afraid. It's about knowing that you will fail sometimes, but that you will get up again and fight for what is honest and true.

Graves Academy doesn't work that way. That place is all about fear and ego. They do what they do out of anger and hate, and that is why ultimately they can never win.

I know that you are worried about the mission tonight. But try to remember, many of the greatest heroes in history were people who weren't the most popular, or the best-looking, or the most powerful. They were just people—people who decided that they would make a difference.

I think you are wonderful, intelligent, and full of potential! When you get back from your mission, I'll treat you to a special trip to Captain Creampuff's, okay?

Love,
Dad

P.S. You forgot the utility belt, so I put it in your top dresser drawer.

She was startled by a knock on her door. Thunderclap and the others entered, chatting animatedly about which villains they might be facing tonight. She quickly hid the letter behind her back.

"Well, there's Blue Ox . . ." Thunderclap looked pointedly at Kibosh. "I'm sure he's hoping to get another shot at you."

Kibosh smacked a leather-gloved fist into his palm. "Bring it on. That guy knocked me into an exotic fish store last week. I still have the piranha bite marks on my leg." He looked ruefully down at his knee. "I owe him one."

"What about Overtime or Dark Mercury? Do you think they'll be there?" Beetlebomb was munching on a glazed donut that was as big as he was.

"Naw, I beat them both last year at that jewelry heist. Can you believe that Overtime guy? He was using his super-speed to steal the change out of a homeless family's cup. Man, that guy is such a loser!"

Thunderclap looked angry.

"All I know is that I have gone unchallenged now since last December."

The Birthday Boy looked relieved. "I really don't like using my weapon if I don't have to."

"Amen to that, brother!" Earthworm was coiled around one of the chairs, his feet resting on the kitchen sink on the other side of the room. "I'll do whatever it takes to try to not let that happen. After you had to use it last time I couldn't sleep for a week! Nightmares every night. Sheesh!"

Summer was sitting quietly on the edge of her bed. She was fighting with terrible insecurity. She didn't have any heroic powers. All of her new friends had heroic abilities and after the classes today she felt more inadequate than ever before.

To make matters worse, a new thought had risen in her mind. What if the reason that she didn't do well at being a hero was because she was in the wrong place? What if she would have done better as a villain at Graves? It made sense in a way. She seemed to be good at ruining things for the heroes at Zoom's. Maybe her destiny was to be the opposite of what these people were? What if a supervillain was just a jealous kid who had never been blessed with looks, popularity, and superabilities?

With these dark thoughts running through her troubled mind, she boarded the shuttle rocket with her friends. They were bound for Megapolis.

...16 THE MISSION

WOMBAT piloted the spaceship through the darkness and soared silently over the twinkling city lights below. He landed the shuttle behind an abandoned factory, which was a block from the art museum, and motioned for the young heroes to group together.

The plan was simple. Kibosh and Earthworm would take the left flank; Beetlebomb and Thunderclap, the right. Birthday Boy would be the lookout and would signal when he spotted the villains entering the building. Summer would stay close to Wombat because this was her first mission.

Time seemed to pass unbearably slowly. Midnight came and went. Summer had a hard time keeping her eyes open. Finally, it was nearing three o'clock in the morning and there was still no sign of any activity. A predawn mist hung over the dewy grass where the heroes maintained their positions.

"Something's not right . . ." Wombat muttered. Suddenly, there was a crackle from Wombat's wrist communicator.

"Academy to Ground Patrol . . ."

Wombat pressed a button. "Go ahead . . ."

"We just received word that there is a robbery in progress at the Scientific Institute. I'm sorry, Jack, but I think you guys were set up."

Wombat wasted no time. "We're on it. Keep me posted about any movement." He shouted to the others. "Back to the shuttle! We're moving out!"

They ran frantically to the shuttle, and with a turbo-charged whine, lifted into the air and rocketed through the city streets.

They arrived at the scene of the crime just in time to see a horde of supervillains lifting a huge wooden crate onto a platform. A black submersible helicopter was hovering over the crate, a large hook descending beneath it to pick up the parcel.

Wombat fired a laser cannon blast into the center of the mob, scattering it in all directions.

Earthworm shouted over the blast, "Better be careful, sir. We don't know what is in that crate!"

"You're roight, Earthworm! Let's land this thing and get to work. Looks like we are outnumbered a little. You kids ready for a fight?"

Everyone but Summer shouted in agreement, and before she knew it, they were on the ground and running toward the fracas.

Summer tried to keep up with Wombat but soon fell behind. A huge spidery kid took a swing at her with one of his eight powerful legs. Summer screamed, ducked, and ran away. She was terrified! She looked everywhere for a place to hide. She finally found an empty planter by a cement stairway and jumped inside.

From her vantage point, she could see everything. Kibosh and a huge kid that she took to be Blue Ox squared off. The ground shook under their colossal blows. Summer winced as Kibosh was struck in his midsection and flew backward, blasting through the window of a pickup truck.

Thunderclap and Overtime smiled grimly at each other, each spotting the other and rocketing together with supersonic speed. They were soon a blur of fists and shouts that careened around the parking lot.

Wombat was magnificent, throwing villains right and left and roaring like a lion.

Summer searched for Beetlebomb. There was a kid dressed in an exterminator's outfit who had Beetlebomb in a glass jar. He was laughing cruelly. The boy almost dropped the jar when there was a tremendous explosion inside the glass. Summer saw quickly that Beetlebomb had apparently detonated himself, but all he succeeded in doing was coating the sides of the jar with a sticky, green goo.

The fighting was getting more heated. Summer made a quick assessment and concluded that they were terribly outnumbered. She watched with apprehension as the helicopter finally managed to hook the crate and was lifting it into the air.

Wombat was now under attack by two villain instructors. An evil iron claw painfully clamped his leg. He was quickly brought to the ground, and blows were raining down on his unprotected head.

Summer trembled. What could she do? She felt completely helpless and terrified. If the fight continued this way, her friends would be captured or killed and all she could do was hide and watch!

"I can't do it." She thought of her dad's letter. "I . . . I can't. I don't have any powers. I'm not like them." She cowered miserably.

Just when all seemed lost, a single low ominous note filled the air. It started softly at first, and then turned into a discordant melody that Summer couldn't immediately place. It grew louder, stronger, filling the air with its horrible sound. Suddenly she heard a voice she knew rising above it, amplified a hundred times. "Happy Birthday to me. Happy Birthday tooo me . . ."

On the outside of the throng, marching slowly and deliberately toward it, was Birthday Boy. His eyes were focused with an unearthly intensity and his hands were pointing at various spots on the ground. Then, what Summer saw next made the hair on the back of her neck stand on end.

Out of the ground rose several misty forms. They had vacant black holes where their eyes should have been, and their tortured wails screeched like fingernails on a chalkboard.

They were the Neverborn. They were the people who were affected by Birthday Boy's fateful wish. Everyone stopped fighting. The villains were momentarily stunned, unable to comprehend this new and terrifying threat. Two of the braver villains sneered and advanced on the spirits. They were quickly overcome.

Summer watched as the wraithlike beings enfolded each one in a deadly embrace. The two students began to age backward. Summer saw the years disappearing as their lives were played in reverse. They were screaming with terror! Soon it was over. They became infants, then embryos, then nothing. The spirits had removed the attackers from existence, making them just like themselves. With a sad expression on his face, Birthday Boy turned to the spot where the two had vanished.

"Come."

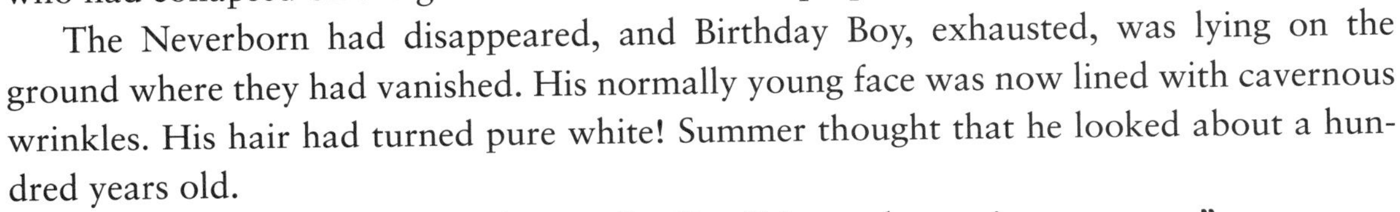

Out of the ground rose the two villains, now wraiths, horrible like the others, and stood behind Birthday Boy awaiting his orders.

Pandemonium broke loose. The panicked villains clambered up ropes to the waiting helicopter and were swiftly carried away, crate and all. Earthworm shot upward after the crate, stretching as fast as he could, but he wasn't fast enough. In a moment they were gone, and the small group was left staring after them.

Summer climbed out of her pot and ran to join the others, who were standing over Birthday Boy, who had collapsed on the ground. Summer wasn't prepared for what she saw next.

The Neverborn had disappeared, and Birthday Boy, exhausted, was lying on the ground where they had vanished. His normally young face was now lined with cavernous wrinkles. His hair had turned pure white! Summer thought that he looked about a hundred years old.

"I'll be all right." He gasped raggedly. "I will be twelve again tomorrow."

Summer watched as Kibosh and Wombat carefully lifted him into the shuttle and laid him in the back on a stretcher.

The ride home was quietly subdued. Summer felt ashamed for hiding. The others didn't say anything, but she knew what they were thinking. She had abandoned them when they needed her most. She stared out of the window, not wanting to look any of them in the eye.

When they arrived back at the dorm, she quickly walked to her cottage and shut the door, not even able to bring herself to say "good night." Embarrassed tears filled her eyes as she climbed into bed.

I'm destined to be a loser. I don't belong here at all! she thought. She let herself cry then. Deep, wracking sobs. She cried because she failed. She cried because of her lack of confidence. Most of all, she cried because deep down inside, she knew that her dad was right about everything, but she couldn't find the courage to be the kind of hero he had mentioned in his letter.

...17
THE ALARM

In the next few days, Summer found that her popularity at Zoom's had reached an all-time low. None of her friends would speak to her. When she ran into Thunderclap in the hallways, they exchanged awkward "Hellos" and moved on.

Oddly enough, the only one who seemed to want to be around her was Tommy Truehart. During the last week, they had arrived in the cafeteria at the same time for lunch, and to Summer's surprise, he would often elect to sit with her, always smiling and friendly.

Today they sat by a large window that overlooked Sof' City. When she had first arrived at Zoom's she had loved to watch the students bouncing off of the side of the marshmallow-styled buildings as they laughed and practiced their newly developed powers. But she felt different now. She hardly noticed the group of Stretchos below who were playing a game of water balloon tag and using their elongated bodies as giant slingshots. All she could think about was Tommy's gentle smile, and it made her feel so embarrassed that she couldn't even make eye contact with him across the table. In the last few days they had talked about their fathers, and as Summer had opened up about the frustrations she had been feeling about her dad, she found that before long her opinions about Jasper were undergoing subtle changes for the worse.

Tommy had secretly confided in her that he and his father had never gotten along, that his father never understood him, and that everyone expected him to be just like him. Summer soon found that she was blaming her dad for her present condition, that all of her problems must have stemmed from her less-than-perfect childhood.

"So, I was thinking . . ." Tommy interrupted Summer's reverie. She glanced up from the window into his smiling face. She bit her lip self-consciously. ". . . I didn't know if you were busy later, but I know this great, uh, place . . ."

Summer noticed that for the first time since they had been meeting in the cafeteria, Tommy seemed uncomfortable. He glanced around nervously and pulled absentmindedly at the stitching in his gloved hand. She wondered what he was getting at. He continued, studying his glove and not meeting Summer's eyes.

"I guess what I'm asking is . . ." He cleared his throat. ". . . Would you like to go out? You know, like on a date or something?" He looked up at Summer with a questioning, vulnerable stare. Summer stared back at him, stunned. Could this be happening? Was Tommy Truehart actually asking her out on an "official" date? She couldn't believe it!

Smiling awkwardly, she managed to squeak out a hoarse "yes" before biting her bottom lip in embarrassment and almost spilling her herbal tea. Tommy grinned broadly.

"Great." He looked around the room, then leaned in slowly and gently put his hand on top of hers. Summer felt as if her heart were going to explode right out of her chest. Tommy lowered his voice.

"Let's not tell anybody, though. You know, let's just keep it special between us, okay?" If she felt at all confused by this request, she didn't show it. All she could do was look at Tommy's handsome, smiling face and nod weakly. Their noses were just inches away from touching. She thought that she had never seen a more beautiful smile in her entire life.

That evening, Summer couldn't wait to get to her dorm and get dressed for her night out. She had long abandoned wearing the outfit that her dad had made for her, and was dressing in the casual clothes she had brought from home. Summer was in front of the mirror, fixing her hair, when there was a soft knock on her door.

"Hey, it's me. Are you in there?"

Summer beamed at the sound of Thunderclap's voice and rushed to open the door.

Thunderclap appeared nervous and shuffled his feet awkwardly as he spoke.

"I haven't seen you around in a while, I just thought . . . well, we haven't really talked since the mission."

He glanced up at her. "Look, the guys and I think you're being too hard on yourself. Everybody fails sometimes, no biggie. You can always have a second chance! I mean, well, we didn't know what to say. I knew you were upset and wanted to give you some space, but we never held it against you. Honest."

Summer didn't care about the failed mission anymore. She was too excited about what had happened at the cafeteria. She smiled broadly.

"Guess what?"

Thunderclap looked confused. "What?"

Summer blurted happily, "I have a date with Tommy!"

Instead of showing any sign of being happy for her, Thunderclap's face darkened. His eyes flashed angrily.

"I've seen you hanging around with him. He's no good, Summer. I'm telling you, he's not really interested in you, he's . . ." But he had gone too far. Summer's mood changed from being happy to angry. What kind of a friend was he anyway? So, what was he saying, that he didn't think she was pretty or popular enough to date Tommy? She felt the familiar resentment she had been experiencing over the last few weeks come rushing back in forceful waves.

"Oh, and how would you know that?" Summer's voice dripped with venom. Thunderclap looked surprised and took an involuntary step backward. She may not have possessed heat vision, but at that moment he thought that her glare was intense enough to melt through solid steel. Her voice grew quiet and dangerous.

"Who *is* good for me? YOU?"

Thunderclap stammered, "I just meant . . . well . . ." But he got no further. Filled with rage and the force of her own emotions, she had slammed the door in his face. Thunderclap waited outside for a full minute, wondering if he should try again. But thinking better of it, he turned, put his hands in his pockets, and walked away.

She found the meeting place that Tommy had described to her shortly after nightfall. It was a beautiful glade with a small bench and a pond. Summer felt excited. She thought back to the first day she had seen him at Foggleberry's.

It just goes to show you that first impressions can be wrong, she thought. *Here I go, thinking he's such a bully and he's really sweet.*

She smiled and looked at her watch. It was seven-thirty. Funny. Tommy was usually early. He had promised to meet her at seven. She looked at the pond. A beautiful swan was swimming nearby. She took the bag of cracker crumbs that Clocksprocket had supplied for her. Feeling full of anticipation for the evening to come, she reached down and offered a handful of crumbs to the swan.

It was so beautiful. Summer admired the graceful bird. Being tame, it allowed itself to be stroked while it nuzzled her palm. Her hand tingled as it ate the crackers.

Suddenly the sound of an alarm split the air. Summer jumped as a searchlight blazed into the night sky displaying a huge letter "Z."

"The emergency signal!" she breathed. She dropped the bag of crumbs and ran back to the campus, heart pounding. The signal could only mean one thing . . . someone had broken into the weakness vault!

In the pond, the swan emerged, waddling over to the spilled bag of crumbs that lay next to the water's edge. It moved with an unnatural awkwardness, for something strange had happened to its feet! They were as large as hubcaps.

At the Administration Building, panicked students were hurriedly taking their assigned places in line directly under the signaling device. Summer quickly took her place. As the alarm finally stopped its piercing scream, the faculty marched solemnly out of the building.

Principal Zoom came last, with

Jasper walking slowly next to him. Summer noticed that her dad looked incredibly agitated. He caught her eye, and then quickly looked away.

"Ladies and gentlemen." Principal Zoom's voice rang above the nervous assembly. "You know why you have been summoned."

A murmur.

"The weakness vault has been broken into and all of the contents have been stolen."

"All of them?" Several panicked voices rustled through the crowd.

"We know who the culprit is, and I can assure you that they will be dealt with in the appropriate manner."

Cries of "who?" echoed through the throng.

"We are fortunate to have a witness who can also corroborate what was taped with the holo cameras. Tommy Truehart arrived on the scene to witness the culprit stealing the contents." Principal Zoom waved a three-fingered hand and a holographic image appeared in the air. Summer gaped openmouthed as she watched the unbelievable footage. The clip showed Summer breaking through the force field of the vault with a laser cannon, then walking through the vault door as if it were made of water, and stealing all of the weaknesses.

Tommy stood up, illuminated by the glow of the signal beam behind him. He pointed at Summer.

"She did it. I saw her." He turned to face the assembly with a look of disgust on his face. "It makes sense, of course, given the fact that her father is Jasper Graves. The brother of our sworn enemy!"

Summer couldn't believe what was happening. Her dad? Her dad couldn't be a villain! NO! *This can't be real!* she told herself.

All eyes turned on Summer. "I . . . I didn't . . . I couldn't . . . I have no powers . . ."

But the words died in her throat. The Elite Guards came and surrounded her, pointing their ray guns threateningly.

She turned to her father.

"Dad, tell them! Tell them that it's a lie!"

Jasper gazed into his daughter's eyes, then looked down, ashamed. Summer stared at him incredulously.

"Then it's true?"

Jasper tried to speak but the guards moved her away, marching her down a hidden corridor to the dark depths below the school. There was a cell, reserved for any captured villains awaiting delivery to the authorities. Summer was guided inside, none too gently, and the door sent crashing behind her.

In a giant, gothic auditorium Hieronimus Graves stood proudly, receiving the thunderous applause from his assembled students and faculty. He paced arrogantly across the stage, framed by giant banners with the school's skull insignia etched upon their surface.

"It has finally been accomplished." His amplified voice boomed loudly, echoing off of the auditorium walls. "Victory is within our grasp. We will mount an attack on Zoom's at midnight tonight and obliterate that cursed school once and for all!"

Cheers.

Graves quieted them with a wave of his hand.

"I formulated the perfect plan. I needed someone to spy for me, someone loyal to our cause. I needed to use my most prized of pupils for the task."

He gestured offstage. To the shock of all, Summer Jones emerged from behind a velvet curtain and walked proudly over to Graves.

The crowd was stunned into silence.

Graves smiled, showing all of his teeth. "Surprised?" He touched Summer's shoulder.

A purple glow emanated from his outstretched arm. Summer's form began to melt, and was replaced by the grinning Tommy Truehart. The crowd gasped in astonishment.

"Using my shape-changing powers I disguised Mr. Truehart so that he could play an important part in my perfectly constructed plan. You see, young Thomas decided that he was tired of everyone expecting him to be just like his 'Old Man,' weren't you, Tommy?"

Tommy looked back at Graves, a smirk on his lips and malice glittering in his eyes.

"When he came to me I welcomed him, and arranged for him to be a double agent, giving him a chance to prove his dedication to our cause. He has proved his immense value twice now . . ."

Graves looked up to an alcove high above, where Captain Truehart's cape hung as a trophy. The assembly broke into uproarious applause.

Graves gestured and turned the applause to Tommy, who bowed slightly to the adoring crowd.

In the darkness below the school, Summer huddled on her small cot. She felt betrayed. *How could he?* she thought. The letter, all that stuff about being a hero. And he was a villain all this time. She couldn't believe it.

But then, maybe this was the secret she feared the most. Maybe this explained everything. Her dad was a villain. Not just any villain, but the brother of Hieronimus Graves. Summer felt an icy hand slip over her heart. Being a villain was her heritage.

She would never be a hero.

. . . 18
HEROES AND VILLAINS

A crack of light blinded her momentarily. She squinted and saw that her dad was being led down the stairway by one of the Elite. They led him to a rocky bench outside of her cell. They didn't say anything for about five minutes. Finally, Jasper broke the silence.

"I was going to tell you . . ."

But he was interrupted by an angry outburst from Summer. "WHEN? When were you going to tell me! You lied to me!"

Her voice cracked. Jasper listened quietly. Summer was shaking all over. Her dad handed her a blanket through the bars. Summer batted it to the floor angrily.

"Why didn't you tell me? Why didn't you? I have spent all my time at this stupid place trying to be something I'm not, and you never told me the truth. That I was destined to be a villain!"

Jasper looked up with a fierce look in his eyes.

"You are NOT a VILLAIN! Just because I was doesn't mean anything!"

He stood up and started to pace.

"I was trying to wait for the right time to tell you. Every time I wanted to, I just couldn't. You are the first. The first in a long line of villains to take the Ring Test and have it glow blue. It has never happened before."

Jasper ran a hand through his hair and sat back down.

"I always hid the fact that I was a supervillain from your mother. I knew that if she ever found out she would leave me. Well, one day she *did* find out. During a robbery I was unmasked and a photographer snapped my picture for the front page. She left me soon after that."

Jasper looked at the floor.

"Six months later I received a phone call. Your mom was pregnant. Deep inside I had always known that being a villain wasn't right, only now, for the first time, I had a reason to change. I decided at that moment that I didn't want you to inherit my legacy. I chose to leave the villains forever."

Summer stared at her father intently. A painful look came over his face.

"My brother and I fought. I almost lost my life, but I escaped. I sought out Principal

Zoom. I had used my powers for evil for so long that they had become something dark and corrupted. So I designed a terrible machine, one that would strip a person of their superhuman abilities. It was the most painful experience I have ever been through. But I gave it all up and became an ordinary mortal."

Jasper looked up at Summer and there were tears shining in his eyes. "I wanted to be a dad that you could be proud of. If I could be one thing, I wanted to be a hero to my daughter."

There was a pause.

Summer got up from the cot and walked to the bars, stretching out her arms to hug her dad. Jasper walked over and they embraced. Jasper knelt down and, holding his daughter's hand, looked her in the eyes. "Destiny has nothing to do with it. Being a hero is a choice. I made that choice thirteen years ago. You can make it too." Summer nodded, tears in her eyes and too happy to speak.

The door at the top of the stairs burst open. Thunderclap came running down the stairs, a piece of paper in his hand.

"I'VE GOT IT! I knew I could figure it out, and I got it!"

Summer wiped her eyes on her sleeve and looked up expectantly.

"You've got what?" Summer asked.

Thunderclap beamed. "I found this book. It's called *Zriggli's Book of Super Abilities.*" He walked up to Summer, showing her the paper.

"I know what your superpower is. It's just like I thought. Totally rare. You are an Enhancer! I kept thinking about what happened at Foggleberry's, you know?"

Jasper and Summer gazed at Thunderclap with confused expressions.

"It means," he continued, "that whoever you touch will have his or her abilities magnified. People with little or no powers could suddenly have one. Somebody already powerful could find themselves like a hundred times more powerful! This power didn't register because it is so rare. There was only one other person in history who ever had it!"

Summer was awestruck. She thought back to what had happened on the soccer field with the boy who did the amazing kick. Tommy, when his powers blazed out of control at the Wonder Mall. Could it be true?

"A superpower Enhancer."

Jasper turned shining eyes upon his daughter.

"Do you realize that this could change the balance of power forever? If your uncle ever found out about this . . ."

Suddenly there was a loud *BOOM!* The cavern shook and rocks started falling everywhere.

"What was that?" Summer asked in a shaky voice. Jasper stared at the ceiling. "It's him. They are attacking."

Thunderclap raced to the door. "It's blocked!" He pulled and strained on the large metal ring. "We're trapped!"

19 ATTACK!

TWO costumed lookouts zoomed through the air back to the campus.

"Attack! Attack! All heroes to arms!"

All students who were wearing civilian clothes rushed into one of the many phone booths that were placed around the school to change into their costumes. Pandemonium reigned as hordes of black ships streaked out of the sky, like a hive of angry hornets, shooting laser beams and fire bolts. Two immense troop-carrying transport ships landed in the center of the campus square. Long ramps extended and soon the black-booted feet of hundreds of Graves students rushed onto the campus, each clutching the box that contained their enemies' weaknesses.

Graves himself followed at the end of the procession on a hovering ebony throne.

"Finally," he whispered, "my moment has come."

Blue Ox gritted his teeth as he clenched the box that contained Kibosh's weakness.

Overtime shot him a cruel grin and, armed with Thunderclap's, sped off to find him.

Exterminator chuckled as he hefted Beetlebomb's box and adjusted his fumigation tanks.

A horribly long, gooey boy held Earthworm's box. "At last, Earthworm will stretch his last!" He made a gargling laugh in his throat and slithered off through the campus.

Finally, Lucifina, the little girl in the black party dress and skull-covered bow, skipped lightly out of the ship, humming the lilting strains of "Happy Birthday."

The students had gathered in the giant hall underneath the Administration Building. Principal Zoom, his eyes glinting like diamonds under his polished goggles, addressed the students.

"They have your weaknesses, so this won't be easy."

A nervous murmur spread through the crowd.

"But we shall not lose hope. You must fight with all of your courage. There is a reason that the heroes prevail and always have."

Principal Zoom's voice rose to a booming crescendo.

"You fight with the conviction that goodness will triumph. We are the heroes of Zoom's Academy. DEFENDERS OF THE WEAK."

There was a small cheer.

"The strong arm of justice."

Louder cheers.

"THE MIGHTY BASTION OF HOPE FOR ALL WHO CALL IN THE TIME OF THEIR GREATEST NEED!"

The crowd was electrified. Resounding cheers echoed around the hall. One by one the troops assembled according to their powers or abilities.

Miss Avian gathered the students together who specialized in flying, and with a mighty battle song they rose into the air. Miss Avian flew at their head, clutching a glittering golden winged banner, leading the streaking procession to war.

The students gifted with incredible strength united under Dynamo, their huge muscles bulging. Many of them roared and bellowed with rage as they stomped off to meet their foes.

Miss Zargovich united the students with mental powers, calling to them telepathically. They nodded in unison without a word and mystically faded from view, using their powers to communicate the status of the war from various locations on the campus.

The groups continued to assemble, the Stretchos, the Speedsters, the Magic Ringers, and lastly the Hodge-Podge, an eager assortment of students with abilities that fit into special categories.

Birthday Boy, pale and determined, twelve years old once again, was in this group. He smiled grimly as he strode out of the building holding a large, carefully wrapped present.

The battle wore on throughout the morning. As the villains were armed with the heroes' weaknesses, the heroes were at a terrible disadvantage. Kibosh rolled on the ground clutching his stomach painfully. His whole appearance had changed. Instead of being big and muscular, he was reduced to a skinny boy in a much-too-baggy costume. Standing over him, leering, was Blue Ox, who held open a box that contained a glittering, jeweled locust.

"Hungry, Kibosh? I'm so sorry, but the grill is closed!" The blue brute guffawed, knowing that the huge boy drew his power from food.

Earthworm faced his nemesis. "So. We meet again, *Snot!*"

The gooey boy smiled a green dripping smile.

"Hello, Worm. *Gurgle.* I brought a little something that you might like to see . . ."

The slimy boy opened the box. Earthworm shouted in dismay as Snot scooped out a white powder and tossed it onto the stretchy boy's skin.

"AAAAGH! MARTIAN SALT!" Earthworm's skin blistered and he fell to the ground, shriveling and weak.

Birthday Boy was steadily sneaking around the perimeter of the evil ships, trying to get to Graves's throne.

"If only they would move!" He gritted his teeth at the number of guards surrounding the evil leader. He noticed that one of the other transport ships was unguarded. He glanced at the present he held. Dashing unseen to the edge of the ship, he quickly undid the bow on top of his box and thrust it inside, diving for cover.

KA-THOOOOOOOM! A huge ball of flame shot into the sky where the ship had been. Birthday Boy watched with grim satisfaction as several villains were engulfed by the blast.

Graves pivoted his throne and spotted him. "SEIZE HIM!"

Birthday Boy was about to start singing the "Birthday Song" when he was interrupted by a shove from behind. He leaped angrily to his feet and saw the girl who stood directly behind him. A look of horror crossed his face. "LUCIFINA!"

The girl smiled prettily. "Why, hello, Hugo. I brought a present for you! Wanna see what's inside?"

Birthday Boy tried to back away but it was too late. Lucifina pulled out a tiny lit candle. "Let's see now . . ." She pursed her lips. "I wish . . ."

...20 ESCAPE

INSIDE Summer's underground prison, Jasper and Thunderclap pounded on the door. Even with Thunderclap's lightning-fast punches it wouldn't budge. They sank back from the door, perplexed and exhausted.

"Wait a minute. I have an idea." Jasper turned to Thunderclap with excitement. "Let's go back over to Summer."

They hurried down the stairs.

"Did it work?" Summer called from her cell below.

"No, but I just thought of something that might."

They gathered outside of Summer's cell.

"Okay, some quick science." Jasper puffed out his cheeks and blew. "When atomic particles are sped up past the speed of light in a solid object, what happens?"

Jasper looked around at their blank expressions.

"Come on!" he said, exasperated. "Think!"

Summer thought a moment, then answered.

"It stops being solid?" She looked at her dad. "What are you getting at?"

"Just this." He looked meaningfully at Thunderclap. "If Thunderclap could run faster than the speed of light, sending shock waves of vibrating energy into the walls of this cavern, we might be able to walk right through them."

"Hey, *yeah!*" Thunderclap's face lit up with dawning realization. "Summer can enhance my powers so that I can run that fast." He turned to Summer. "You ready to give it a try?"

Summer didn't know what to think. She didn't feel any different than before. What if it didn't work?

She looked at her dad's and Thunderclap's excited faces. She knew she had to try. She thought back to the two other times that something had happened with her power. She remembered the "tickling spider" sensation she felt when her hand rested on the boy's shoulder in the soccer game.

"I'm not exactly sure how I made it work."

Summer reached over to Thunderclap.

"But I made contact with Tommy in Foggleberry's, and my hand touched the shoulder of the kid at the soccer game."

Thunderclap let Summer rest her hand on his shoulder. Nothing happened.

After a few minutes of trying Summer got frustrated.

"It's not working!"

Thunderclap pondered for a moment. "Sometimes to activate powers you need a trigger. For me, I have to think fast . . . literally."

He looked at Summer. "Try again, but this time try to feel like you felt the last time you can remember something happening."

Summer thought back, searching for anything that might have been in common with the other two occasions. When she had fallen to the ground in the soccer game, she remembered feeling like the boy who tackled her was a much better player than she was.

In Foggleberry's she was afraid when she had bumped into Tommy, afraid because he seemed so powerful. Suddenly she remembered a more recent time when she had felt the tickling sensation in her hand. When she was feeding the swan at the pond.

She had been thinking that the swan was one of the most graceful swimming birds she had ever seen.

"Maybe it's when I feel really strongly about someone's abilities being extra powerful." Summer looked meaningfully at Thunderclap. "Let's try again."

She reached through the bars and touched his shoulder. She concentrated, trying to feel something. The first thing that came to mind was how she felt when she saw how fast Thunderclap had run the mile, setting a new record for the school. How she had thought he was so amazingly fast, and had admired his ability. She focused, trying to make him even faster in her mind. He was faster than an airplane, faster than the wind! She pictured atomic particles racing away into infinity, all within a single ray of sunlight.

Suddenly the tickling feeling began to spread down her fingers.

"I . . . whoa . . . *I think it's working!*"

Thunderclap started vibrating with uncontrolled energy. He gasped, his eyes widening with amazement.

Suddenly he took off! There was a sonic boom. Then he was a blur, flashing around the room almost invisibly. Then he was gone. Summer gave her dad a huge, amazed smile.

The next thing they knew, the walls and bars became semitransparent.

"Quick, follow me!" Summer and her dad rushed right through the cave wall, and up to the surface, where a terrible sight met their eyes.

...21
TO THE RESCUE!

FROM their vantage point behind one of the Sof' City buses, they could see hundreds of bodies of disempowered faculty and students littering the once-beautiful campus. A jeering horde of students accompanied by Phydeux and Crimson Claw was kicking the crumpled forms of Mr. Fleet and Dynamo. Miss Avian, her cape in tatters and looking weak and pale, stared defiantly back at the snaky form of Slithestra, who was rearing back to strike with her poison fangs. Villainous students were everywhere, destroying everything that they could get their hands on.

"Man, are they going to pay for this one!" Thunderclap appeared and smacked his fist into his palm. He was starting to march over to the villains when Jasper held him back.

"Wait. We need a plan."

After a quick assessment, it was decided that Thunderclap would use his newly enhanced speed to lure the villains away from the fallen heroes and try to steal back the weaknesses. Meanwhile, Summer would attend to the fallen, enhancing their powers and reviving them once again.

"What about Graves?" Thunderclap and Summer looked at Jasper, who looked grim and determined.

"It's about time my brother and I had a little talk."

Thunderclap strode out to the wildly celebrating villainous mob. He put his hand on Tommy Truehart's shoulder and, pretending to laugh, asked what the "big joke" was. Tommy's eyes widened with shock as he realized who it was.

"YOU!"

"Yeah. Me. Oh, and by the way, this is for what you did to Summer . . ."

Thunderclap reared back and delivered a hundred explosive, lightning-fast punches before Tommy could land a single one. Tommy slumped to the ground, unconscious. The villainous horde stared at Thunderclap with disbelief.

Thunderclap spotted Overtime and Dark Mercury. He walked over and tapped them on the shoulders. "Tag. You're it." The mob let out a collective roar.

"HE'S MINE!" shouted Overtime, and the entire mob gave chase. Thunderclap rushed into a nearby building, the others trailing far behind him.

When Overtime arrived inside, he paused to open Thunderclap's weakness chest. Thunderclap, still enhanced by Summer's powers, whisked it out of his hands. Each of the other villains stared stupidly at thin air, stunned, as they suddenly found their hands empty. Thunderclap, his arms full with the stolen weakness chests, chuckled mockingly at Overtime from across the room. He smiled to himself. He didn't even feel winded.

"Man, that was awesome."

He was so busy admiring his handiwork that he didn't notice the giant wooden hand that crashed through the window and gripped him in its gigantic palm, practically crushing his ribs. The earth fell away as Thunderclap rose into the air and stared, wide-eyed, into the terrible face. Now, standing fifty feet tall, there was Kapu. Red-hot lava dripped from his gaping maw. Hissing steam escaped from between his teeth as he smiled his terrible smile.

"I SHALL FEAST!" he gloated, and Thunderclap helplessly watched as he was lifted toward the giant's crushing jaws.

Everything seemed to happen quickly for Summer after the three had separated. She rushed around the campus, enhancing everybody who she could reach. She was amazed to see Dynamo, her muscle-bound instructor, leap to his feet with twice as many bulging muscles as before. Miss Avian sprouted glittering hydrofoil wings out of her back, and took off, soaring into the sky. When she reached Birthday Boy she found that somebody had removed his mouth! She quickly revived him and all of her other friends and faculty, all of them amazingly enhanced beyond their wildest dreams.

They regrouped into formation, and under Summer's direction, searched for the villains who had chased Thunderclap.

She was reviving her last student, a little pixie of a girl named Emily, when she spotted Thunderclap being held by the fifty-foot tiki god.

"Oh, no!" She looked around. There was nobody around to help her. She was about to panic, her old fears of inadequacy rushing upon her, when she suddenly remembered the conversation she had had with her dad a few moments before.

She steeled her nerve and looked at her surroundings. Her dad, being ever resourceful, had always told her, "Solutions to problems can sometimes be right in front of you, you just have to know how to look." She began searching for something, anything that might help her figure out a way to rescue Thunderclap. She noticed a big, broad-rimmed yellow hat lying next to a battered phone booth. Summer's mind raced, trying to figure out why it looked familiar. Suddenly it all came rushing back. The Mysterious Snazzoo! The word he had whispered in her ear on that first day in the Wonder Mall! Somehow she knew that it was meant to be used at precisely this moment. Now, if she could just find a way to get to Thunderclap she could say it and . . .

She mechanically began searching her pockets. She felt something flat and hard in her back pocket. She reached back and pulled out a brass card with tiny holes punched into it. "Clocksprocket!" she breathed excitedly.

She searched the area and soon found one of the little summoning booths that the robot had told her to use if she needed him. It was bent at the base, but appeared to be in working condition. Summer slid the card inside and waited.

He arrived sooner than she had expected. In moments, she heard clanking rushing over the hill as fast as the metal man's brass legs would carry him.

"*Click. Whirr.* You called, miss?"

"I need your help, can you fly? My friend is in trouble!"

The little robot paused. Summer waited for his answer. Then she gaped as something strange happened to his dimly glowing eyes. They began flashing brightly in a mathematical sequence . . . yellow . . . blue . . . yellow . . . white . . . yellow. Two yellows. Two blues. Three yellows. Clocksprocket's head whirled on its base. His hands reached up to remove it and with lightning speed began to reassemble his entire body into something different. In a flash it was done. A gleaming brass jet pack lay on the ground at Summer's feet.

Without hesitation Summer picked it up. It was surprisingly light, and she strapped it on her back. She looked up, high into the sky, where Thunderclap was suspended, directly above the idol's gaping mouth.

"Hang on! I'm coming!" she shouted as she punched the green button that flashed on the belt around her waist. Hardly having time to catch her breath, she was swept upward with a tremendous roar and force that resembled a racetrack filled with Formula One cars. Like her father's rocket, she shot into the sky, flying toward her goal with jetlike speed.

Thunderclap's eyes widened with fear as Kapu's grip tightened. The idol's fiery gaze narrowed and he began to laugh, a horrible, raspy sound like two pieces of gigantic sandpaper being rubbed together. Thunderclap could see that the wooden god was fully enjoying his moment of villainous triumph.

"Please, just get it over with," he begged desperately to himself as the huge fist that held him lowered itself to the steaming, wooden jaws. Suddenly the idol stopped his hand midway to his mouth, and brought the boy back up to eye level. Like so many of the villains Thunderclap had encountered, the tiki couldn't resist gloating over his triumphs.

"Foolish mortal," the ancient god thundered. "I can see by the look in your eyes that you think your pitiful life is somehow worth saving." Thunderclap gagged on the sulfurous fumes that swept from the giant's mouth. The god snapped the huge tree-trunk fingers on the hand that wasn't holding Thunderclap and the air around them immediately fell into an unearthly stillness. Moments later, a feeling of static electricity began to grow, and Thunderclap's eyes widened as the little hairs on the back of his arms, wrists, and neck stood on end.

Then there was a windy howl as heavy, black storm clouds gathered and circled slowly above them. For a split second hope flared inside of Thunderclap as he saw the jagged green lightning, but the feeling was gone as quickly as it came when he realized that even if he had his super-speed it wouldn't be enough to break the massive iron grip that held him fast. The evil tiki seemed to grow even bigger as the thunder crackled around his massive head.

Kapu laughed and continued his indulgent rant.

"You should feel honored, insignificant one!" he hissed. Thunderclap noticed the deadly lava dribbling down the idol's rotten teeth.

"There was a time when hundreds of my followers were sacrificed day and night just to appease my wrath." The wooden giant tightened his grip a bit more. Thunderclap felt as if his ribs were being slowly crushed. The tiki's eyes glowed with a greedy red light. From somewhere, the sound of creepy tribal drumming and chanting filled the air. Thunderclap panicked, thinking that a lack of oxygen was affecting his brain and making him hear things! But then he noticed, somewhat relieved, that there was a speaker with wires tucked neatly inside of a small box protruding from behind the giant's left ear. The arrogant idol had come equipped with his own villainous sound track for the occasion! Thunderclap grimaced.

Why do they always have to get so theatrical?

The massive hand rose through the air and dangled him above the tiki's gaping mouth like a cat about to drop a dainty, feathered morsel into its empty stomach.

Suddenly, just as he could feel the giant's fingers loosen, there was a tremendous, booming shout behind him. It was a familiar voice that was shouting a strange and ancient word.

"MAKALAMANU!"

The idol froze. Summer, her hair whipping wildly in the heavy winds, was hovering slightly above Kapu's right ear. Her eyes flashed with storms that looked twice as angry and powerful as the ones that the tiki god had been able to conjure. Kapu was speechless. Then, slowly, the giant's face collapsed like an ancient ruin.

"How did you know?" he rumbled feebly.

Suddenly the wood was splintering into a thousand pieces. The giant roared with dismay as his legs crumbled beneath him.

Summer caught Thunderclap in midair and rocketed to safety, wooden shards exploding with a tremendous *BOOM!* behind them as they swept down to the ground.

When they landed, Thunderclap gazed at Summer in admiration as she unbuckled the smoking jet pack.

"Wow. So much for your fear of heights, huh?"

Summer was about to reply when they were interrupted by a nearby commotion. An evil batlike creature was racing through the air with leathery wings flapping, followed by the few villainous students who were still able to fly.

As the figure raced by he caught sight of Summer and dove down, grabbing her by the ankle. Summer screamed as she was suspended high above the earth. A voice, rough as sandpaper, called down to her.

"Now, now, is that any way to greet your dear old uncle?"

Her stomach clenched in fear and anger.

"Let me go!" she shouted into the whistling breeze.

"It is time you embraced your destiny, my dear. You will be even greater than your father ever was!"

Summer fought against her uncle's grip with all of her might.

"I make my own choices, *Uncle!*"

Suddenly an object hit Graves in the side of the head with a bone-crushing *CRACK!* The jet-powered boomerang made a beautiful swoop and returned to earth, landing in Jasper's outstretched hand.

"PUT HER DOWN!" Summer heard her father's voice booming from below. He sounded furious.

Graves let out a scorching hiss, and dropped Summer.

She screamed as the earth rushed up at her. Flashing thoughts raced through her head. If only she hadn't removed Clocksprocket's jet pack! She was just about to hit the earth when an enormous pair of springy hands caught her and bounced her gently back into the air like a trampoline. It was Earthworm. Summer didn't have time to thank him. She jumped to the ground and hurried to her dad, who was squaring off with his evil brother. If only she had thought of it sooner! Maybe she could have enhanced him!

Graves let out a growl, and shot toward his brother, screaming with rage. Jasper stood his ground, armed only with his boomerang, a peaceful calm on his face. Graves began to morph in midair, his outstretched arms becoming long, glittering silver spikes.

It was over far too quickly. Summer screamed as she saw Graves's spikes pierce her father and take him to the ground with a lethal blow. The faculty raced to attack, but Graves had already flown, his evil laugh echoing behind him.

Summer rushed to her dad's side. She was barely conscious of a constant screaming coming from somewhere, but didn't realize that it was coming from her own lips. She put her hands on her father's shoulders, trying to will her powers into him. A tattered and war-torn Principal Zoom rushed over and called for the medical team. Suddenly the earth started moving under Summer's feet and everything went dark. She didn't feel anything when she hit the ground.

. . . 22
SUMMER'S CHOICE

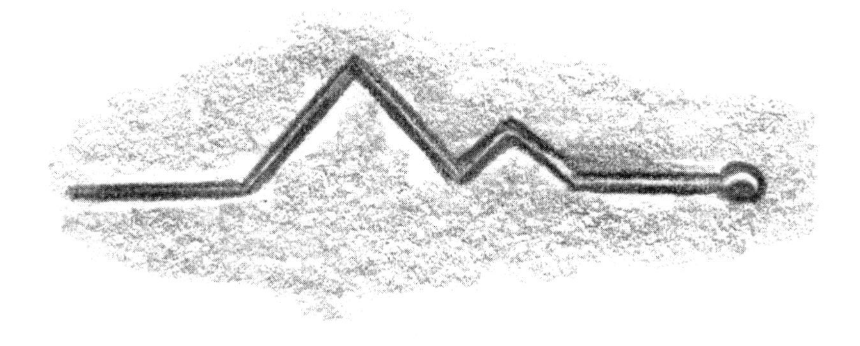

WHEN Summer awoke, she was lying in her bed back at the dorm tree. The anxious faces of her friends were gathered around her.

"Hey, guys! She's waking up!"

Beetlebomb's high buzzing voice echoed from above her. Kibosh, Earthworm, Birthday Boy, and Thunderclap looked pale and worried. Summer tried to sit up.

"Where's my dad?"

The boys exchanged furtive glances.

"*Where is he?*" Summer tried to fight down the panic that was still racing inside of her. Thunderclap reached out a gentle hand.

"Principal Zoom admitted him to the hospital wing. I'm sorry, Sum, but . . ." Thunderclap hesitated, a choky sound coming out of his voice. "It doesn't look good."

Summer shakily got out of bed and put her coat on.

"Take me to him."

The boys exchanged nervous glances, but something in Summer's voice made them obey without question.

Principal Zoom met Summer outside of her dad's intensive care room. Summer thought he looked like he was a thousand years old. She rushed to him and asked how her dad was doing. The professor sighed deeply.

"I'm afraid that we have done all that we can." He moved over to the pale-faced Summer and took her arm.

"Your father is between life and death. I am certain that without intervention he will die."

Summer's heart caught in her throat. Tears welled up in her eyes.

"You said, 'without intervention,' what do you mean?" She choked.

"I can think of only one possible way to bring your father back, but it is risky, and might not work."

The little professor rubbed his hands together anxiously.

"Your father used to possess a very rare gift. His body could heal itself from almost any damage done to it. It was what made him such a formidable foe."

He looked at Summer with an intense stare.

"The machine that he made to take his powers away was capable of one other task. It could permanently transfer superpowers from one person to another. It is my guess . . .

and only a guess, mind you . . . that if your powers were transferred to your father it might provide him with the ability to tap into the powers that were taken from him and allow his body to heal itself."

Summer's heart leaped. "What do I have to do?"

Principal Zoom held up a cautionary finger. "You must realize that this might mean the complete loss of your powers. I don't know if it will even work. And to make matters worse, only your father knew how to operate the machine."

At this the professor took Summer's hands in his own.

"You are the only one who can make this decision. We were hoping that maybe because you are his daughter you might be able to figure out how the machine works. Think carefully about this, Summer. Your decision now could change your life forever."

Summer thought of her dad, making the choice to undergo so much pain to leave the villains to be a hero to her. She glanced around at the hallway where they stood. Pictures of many of the past graduates from Zoom's were hanging on the wall. For the first time she felt like she belonged at Zoom's. She turned to the professor with a look of pale determination.

"Show me where to go. I'm ready."

...23 HER FATHER'S DAUGHTER

IN a secret room behind Principal Zoom's bookcase was the machine. It was full of black steel, gears, and wicked-looking glass containers. Summer could immediately see why nobody knew how to work it, for it was full of complex twists and turns of metal that would baffle anybody.

Maybe Dad intended it that way, she thought to herself. He had told her that losing his powers had been a painful process. It would be like him to not want anyone to use it needlessly. She looked at the machine carefully and tried to think of all of her father's countless inventions. She had grown up with them. Some of the safer ones had even been toys. She remembered one in particular; it was like a hoop within a hoop that would hover endlessly on its base. She used to stare at it constantly when she was little, and had called it her "Loopy-thingy." She remembered that her dad was proud of his work, and always made a little mark on the bottom of each piece. A mark that looked just like . . .

Summer saw the familiar shape of a quarter moon on the underside of one of the panels on the machine. She called to the professor.

"Get the holding tanks ready, Professor, I found it."

Moments later, Summer was suspended in a large hovering capsule next to her father, who looked terribly pale and unconscious. Miss Avian assisted Principal Zoom in preparing them both, tightly sealing the doors to the pods within which they were floating.

Summer had shown Principal Zoom the switch, and he was in position, waiting for Summer's signal that she was ready.

Summer looked out of the semitransparent glass to the room below her. Funny. She didn't feel afraid anymore. She looked lovingly over at her father, then back to Principal Zoom, and nodded.

A low rumbling filled the chamber. Sparks flew as fiery energy burst forth from the spinning centrifuge. Summer cried out in pain as a glowing fluid began flowing from her arm and was transfused into her father.

A musical hum began to build. The room shook. Soon the single note was a harmonious crescendo that sounded like a hundred church organs playing a majestic chord! Gears spun madly on their axes, the metal works strained to bursting! Glass bulbs shattered in a shower of electrical sparks, dancing across the floor like crackling bolts of lightning. It looked as if the machine were about to fly apart!

Suddenly everything slowed. The music died down to a discordant hum. Principal Zoom and Miss Avian rushed to unlock the chamber doors.

Summer fell forward with a gasp. So much pain! She was amazed that she was still alive. She gasped raggedly, and asked Miss Avian to check on her father.

Principal Zoom unlocked Jasper's chamber door. As the smoky glass was opened, a radiant golden glow illuminated the professor's stunned alien face.

Jasper stepped from the chamber. His body was covered in beautiful silver armor, the glow coming from a golden, winged "Z" that shone proudly from his chest. Summer gazed weakly over at her dad and smiled. He was alive.

Jasper dashed over to his daughter anxiously. He wheeled on Principal Zoom, demanding to know how they could subject his daughter to this infernal machine!

"It was her choice, Jasper." Principal Zoom looked at Summer with admiration. "I would be hard-pressed to say that I have ever seen a more heroic act"—he looked back at Jasper and smiled—"if I hadn't known about a similar one that somebody else once did."

Jasper gazed down at his daughter, his eyes brimming with tears.

"It's all right, Dad," Summer weakly replied, "I would rather have you than superpowers anyway." Jasper knelt and embraced his daughter, tears flowing down his cheeks.

Miss Avian silently watched the two, her own eyes shining. Principal Zoom patted her back, and was about to say something, when his attention was drawn to a blinking monitor.

He gazed down at it and chuckled wonderingly.

He walked over to Jasper and Summer, asking Miss Avian to join him.

"Summer, would you please take Miss Avian's hand?"

Summer, feeling too weak to protest, gave him a tired, inquisitive look, then reached slowly over and touched Miss Avian's outstretched hand.

The room was silent.

Suddenly Summer's hand began to glow. Miss Avian, her eyes round with surprise, gasped as glittering hydrofoil wings once more extended out of her back. Jasper looked at them incredulously.

"But . . . how?"

"Apparently"—Principal Zoom's eyes twinkled underneath his goggles—"the machine only removes corrupted powers. I believe that it makes a very convincing case that heroic powers are firmly planted in the hero."

He walked over to Summer and laid a gentle hand on her shoulder. "And that they never die."

...24
THE COMIC BOOK

THREE months later one-hundred-foot-tall banners decorated the outside of the newly repaired Academy buildings. Principal Zoom ordered the construction of a mammoth stage in the center of Speedy Stadium for a special ceremony. The entire school was abuzz, eager to attend the special event.

When the momentous evening finally arrived, everyone showed up dressed in his or her best costume. Summer had had her hair done up especially for the occasion by Clocksprocket, who was now a proud member of the Elite Guard. He had been whirring and clicking proudly since he had been elected, and shined the newly glittering "Z" on his chest so often that he was running low on brass polish.

Thunderclap showed up for Summer at precisely 7:00 A.M., his new outfit gleaming brightly. Summer blushed as he offered his arm, and they walked to the stadium together, talking in low voices.

On an immense platform in the brightly lit arena, Principal Zoom quieted the chattering assembly with a gentle wave of his three-fingered hand.

"Ladies and gentlemen. We are gathered here tonight for a special occasion, one that happens very seldom for this school."

The crowd waited with hushed anticipation. Summer held Thunderclap's hand, her heart beating wildly.

"As you know, the highest honor that Zoom's Academy can bestow on an alumna is immortalizing him or her in our chosen medium of communication. The comic book."

The crowd murmured appreciatively.

"The comic book is often underestimated in its power. Many fail to realize that it is through this medium that we have the ability to influence young people around the world to make heroic choices." He looked around the packed stadium meaningfully.

"This year, our candidate is unlike any other. To begin with, this student is not a graduate."

Excited whispers rustled through the stadium. This had never happened before!

"The student that we the faculty have elected this year has shown exceptional abilities. The student has shown courage in the face of the most extreme danger, and self-sacrifice beyond what is typical even among some of the past recipients of this award."

The student body held its collective breath as Principal Zoom was handed a golden envelope that would announce the winner. Summer looked around the stadium, wondering who this "hero of heroes" might be. She glanced at Thunderclap out of the corner of her eye. He was staring at the envelope with an eager expression on his face.

"I hope it's him," she murmured under her breath, thinking how happy the award would make him. The crowd was hushed as Principal Zoom read the announcement, his eyes twinkling.

"Miss Summer Jones. Would you please come forward?"

Summer stared openmouthed at the stage. Had she heard him correctly? Excited hands were patting her on the back. Thunderclap helped her to her feet as the loud "whoops" from Kibosh, Earthworm, Beetlebomb, and Birthday Boy echoed loudly behind her.

She walked to the stage amid deafening cheers. The faculty seated behind Principal Zoom applauded as Summer was presented with a comic book that depicted her on the cover, racing skyward with a jet pack strapped to her back.

Summer looked across the stage to her father, who was beaming with pride, his new armor shining brightly. Suddenly she felt a gloved hand upon her shoulder and heard a whisper in her right ear. She barely had time to see who it was, for the figure wearing a broad-brimmed hat leaped quickly from the stage and swept invisibly into the cheering crowd. This time the word that he had given her was a word that she knew. It was a word that she had heard before but had never believed about herself.

Miss Avian's students shot into the sky and flew in a glittering formation around the tower. Students with the power to control fire and water caused an amazing hydro-pyrotechnic display that Summer was sure would be a featured part of this year's Zoom's Academy Yearbook.

She gazed around the stadium at the happy, cheering faces and knew that she was one of them. She belonged. And a mysterious someone had told her that there was a word for what she now was.

She was a hero.

SUMMER
10¢

EPILOGUE

*C*LIP, *clip, clip, clip.* The booted feet of Hieronimus Graves paced restlessly in front of a huge mirror in his secret chamber.

There was a knock at the chamber door.

"Enter."

"Greetings, Your Excellency."

Tommy Truehart, having abandoned his Zoom's costume for one that was completely black, stood rigidly at attention, his eyes carefully avoiding Graves's hideous features.

Graves stopped his pacing to cast an appraising eye on him.

"I want you to inform Fiend and Slithestra that we have a new plan. We will focus all of our efforts on the capture of Summer Jones."

Tommy shifted his feet uncomfortably.

"Sir, if I may ask, how is that possible? I mean, she will be too well guarded, won't she?"

Graves, his back turned to Tommy, laughed softly.

"Idiot," he whispered. "You have yet to learn that nothing is truly impossible."

Tommy watched with a stunned expression as Graves's form began to melt, his face twisting and morphing into something else entirely. It was over in a matter of seconds.

"I'm sorry I ever doubted you, sir."

Graves turned to inspect his new features, now bearing the familiar smiling face of Jasper Jones.

THE CAPTURE . . . OF THE . . . CRIMSON CAPE

For Alex and Olivia

CONTENTS

THE CAPTURE . . . OF THE . . . CRIMSON CAPE

. . . 1 BIG NEWS

"WHAT do you mean, you're getting married?" Summer stared at her father in disbelief. Jasper, looking a bit uncomfortable, grasped a steaming mug of coffee from Captain Creampuff's Bakery in his gray-gloved hands.

"I know it's a surprise. But, Sum, I think it's going to be really good for all of us." He took a gulp of scalding coffee, winced, then continued.

"You do like Betty, right? After all, she's crazy about you." Her father's eyes twinkled.

Betty Avian, "Miss Avian" to Summer, had been seeing her dad for a while now. Summer liked her, and had gotten to know her better while she had spent much of the break from school at their house in Thousand Oaks, California.

Initially, Summer thought that it had been kind of weird to see her in her street clothes. She had only known Miss Avian as the Flying Instructor at Zoom's Academy, where she wore pink tights with a winged symbol emblazoned on her chest. When she was over at their house she wore jeans and sweaters and looked so normal that prior to going to Zoom's, Summer would have never believed that the thirty-year-old woman possessed "superpowers."

When Summer saw her dad and Betty kiss for the first time it had made her feel like she swallowed something too big for her stomach. She had never seen her dad kiss anybody since the divorce, and it was still kind of awkward and hard to get used to.

It wasn't that Betty wasn't nice. She was. The thing that bothered Summer the most about the news, besides the fact that her dad was marrying somebody other than her mom, was the fact that Betty had a son that Summer thought was the most annoying kid in the whole world.

Dennis Avian was nine years old and was very proud of the fact that he was an authority on every comic book hero ever invented. When Summer had visited the Avians' house for the first time, Dennis had wasted no time introducing her to his extensive comic book collection.

In fact, Summer thought, "collection" wasn't even the proper word. "Obsession" was more like it. She had suffered through three hours of Dennis talking about his favorite hero, Captain Truehart, and had been bored to tears as he paged through example after example of Truehart's comic book exploits in each of his two hundred forty-three issues, talking breathlessly about every villain he had ever defeated, every superpower that he possessed, and how anybody who didn't agree with him was "just stupid."

Her dad and Dennis got along really well, which made Summer twinge with jealousy. Jasper had been close friends with Captain Truehart, and whenever Dennis came over he spent much of his time riddling her dad with questions about what it had been like to hang out with "the captain." Jasper, always happy to talk about his heroic friend, found a rapt and attentive audience. And Summer knew that if there was one thing her dad loved to do, it was to tell nostalgic stories about the "glory days" of heroes.

The Avians' last visit had been especially bad. Summer had been in her room with the door closed, practicing her superpowers. Last year at Zoom's she had been tested and it was discovered that she had a very rare gift. She was only the second "Enhancer" in Zoom's illustrious history.

A Superpower Enhancer was somebody who possessed no specific powers of their own, but by making contact with someone or something else, could cause any powers that they already possessed to be doubled or even tripled in strength! Her powers of Enhancement had proved to be the key to thwarting an attempt by the villainous students of Graves Academy from destroying Zoom's completely, and Summer had been rewarded for her role in saving the school by being presented with the highest honor the school could bestow: She had been immortalized in the pages of her own comic book.

She was slowly getting used to her newfound powers and still felt a little insecure about practicing them publicly. She couldn't always make them work, especially when she was feeling angry or upset and was trying to get the hang of concentrating on the images necessary to activate them.

On Dennis's last visit, Summer had been in her room working on her powers with Nelson, her tabby, the laziest cat ever. In fact, Nelson had gotten so fat and demanded to be fed so often that he had taken to wearing his food bowl on top of his head like a hat and slowly waddled around the house with it perched crookedly over one eye while mewing loudly for a snack every five minutes.

Summer felt that something had to be done about her feline's eating disorder so she decided that trying to use her powers to enhance his metabolism might help him work off a few pounds.

She had been deep in concentration with her hand stroking Nelson's fur, trying to activate her powers, when the bedroom door burst open and Dennis came marching into the room, grinning broadly.

"Hi, Summer!"

Summer had grunted a sulky "hullo."

"I just finished reading your first issue." He jumped unceremoniously upon the edge of her bed. After not getting any response from her, his face lost its eager expression and had turned nonchalant. He had sniffed imperiously and said, "I thought it was just so-so."

She noticed that he held her only copy of her comic book, the first issue of *Summer,* in his left hand.

Summer rolled her eyes and tried her best to ignore him. She said nothing and returned her concentration to her cat. Unfortunately, she was too annoyed to be able to get her powers to work. Dennis on the other hand did not pick up the hint and took her silence as cause to continue.

"Captain Truehart wouldn't have wasted as much time as you did trying to figure out how to rescue Thunderclap Collins from the evil tiki god. He would have just flown up and smashed him to splinters with one punch."

Summer gritted her teeth in annoyance.

"Well, Captain Truehart wasn't there, was he?"

Captain Truehart, Zoom's Academy's greatest hero, had died protecting the Academy from her evil uncle, Hieronimus Graves, just prior to Summer starting the previous year.

Tommy Truehart, the captain's son, had resented the fact that everyone at the school expected him to live up to his father's legacy and had consequently turned traitor, betraying the school and joining the villains' side, but not before tricking Summer into believing that he was interested in dating her.

For Summer, that had been the part that hurt the most. She had never had anybody "interested" in her before and had fallen for the handsome boy's clever ruse. While spending time with Tommy, Summer had gotten blamed for a crime she didn't do and was almost expelled from Zoom's Academy forever.

Dennis grabbed one of Summer's pillows and tossed it up in the air and punched it across the room, where it crashed into her Gothic Girl alarm clock and knocked it to the floor. Without noticing, Dennis turned to Summer.

"Well, it's too bad that Captain Truehart wasn't there. You were lucky that you had that stupid robot to help you out or you would have been toast!"

Maybe it was because Dennis had "touched a nerve" with some of her insecurities about not having any particular powers of her own, or perhaps it was because the incident with the tiki god had spiraled into events that had almost gotten her dad killed, but Summer was suddenly filled with icy rage. She jumped to her feet and gave the smaller boy a hard push.

"I almost lost my dad in that battle, you little creep." Summer's voice had trembled with anger. "You have no idea what that is like and have no right to say anything about it."

The push had knocked Dennis back, but that wasn't what had done the damage. His face had suddenly clouded over, and had gotten the tight, pinched expression of someone who was trying not to cry. Carefully avoiding Summer's gaze, he stood up and stalked out of her room.

When she emerged from her room a few minutes later, the Avians had gone. Her dad wore a stern expression as he called her over to the living-room couch and told her that Dennis's own father had died three years ago and that he was still having a hard time getting over it.

Summer knew that she should feel worse about saying what she had said to the boy. She felt bad about hurting Dennis's feelings, but was wrestling with so many frustrated feelings of her own about him that she felt only a little guilty about not being more compassionate. Something about the fact that her dad was "sticking up" for him made her feel

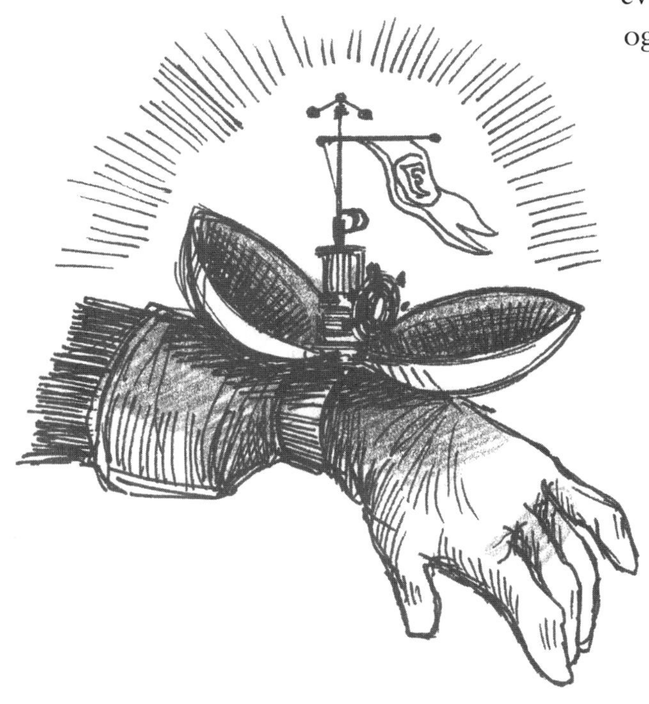

even more resentful. She had mumbled an apology and left the room, wanting to be left alone.

Now, as she sat across from her dad at Captain Creampuff's Bakery and had just been told that Dennis was going to be her new stepbrother, she was speechless.

BRRRRIIIIIIIP! Click, clunk. WHIIIRRR! The strange brass contraption Jasper wore on his wrist and called a "watch" began spinning furiously. Suddenly the egg-shaped dial split in two, and a small flag unfurled with a message printed across its surface in silver letters.

"Hmm. It's from Foggleberry. Wonder what he could want?" Jasper stood up and gave Summer an awkward half hug.

"We can talk some more after school lets out, okay? Betty and Dennis will be joining us for dinner at Zanzibar's tonight and we can all celebrate!"

Summer watched as he grabbed one of the brass poles that stretched down from the ceiling to a hole in the floor, and slid downstairs. As Summer stared after him she realized that once again, her whole world was about to change.

"Why does this keep happening to me?" she whispered sadly as she stood up and walked slowly over to the elevator and pushed the down button.

"ONE hundred forty-three, one hundred forty-four, one hundred forty-five . . ."

Dennis Avian carefully slid each of his precious *Captain Truehart* comics into a protective sleeve with cardboard backing. As he did so, he counted the issue numbers quietly to himself.

Today was a very big day. Last week, his mom had given him a special ring to put on, a ring that glowed with a steady blue light when she had placed it on his finger. Dennis had waited a very long time for that to happen. He knew exactly what it meant. The "Ring Test" was the only way a person could find out if they had superpowers, and only if it glowed blue could they go to Zoom's Academy.

His mom had made a big deal about it and was really excited, but for Dennis it hadn't come as much of a surprise. He knew he had superpowers. He had even practiced them once in a while when nobody was looking.

He smiled to himself as he got to number "one hundred fifty."

Most of the students at Zoom's started their training when they were around twelve, but Dennis had begged his mom to test him early. It wasn't often that superpowers showed up in someone as young as he was, but he had always felt like he was special. Destined. He knew that he was going to be great someday. Maybe even as great as Captain Truehart himself.

He gazed with satisfaction at the neatly packed box and taped the cardboard lid firmly in place. His mom was busy loading the last of their luggage into the invisible zeppelin they kept in the backyard. Dennis's comics had certainly taken up a large portion of the cabin, but there was no way in the world he could conceive of leaving a single issue behind.

"DENNY, WE'RE LEAVING! I NEED YOU OUT HERE PRONTO!"

His mom's shout floated in to him from the backyard.

"COMING, MOM! ONE SEC!"

He quickly scribbled the issue numbers onto a small label and placed it carefully on the edge of the box. Then, grunting with the effort, he hefted the box out his bedroom door.

The sun had just melted into the grassy mountains behind their small house and early evening stars twinkled in the hazy twilight. A light wind ruffled through Dennis's jet-black hair as he boarded the transparent blimp and disappeared from sight.

This is gonna be great, he thought as he put the box down on top of the huge pile and collapsed into the co-pilot's seat next to his mother.

Miss Avian gave her son's ear a friendly tweak before pulling back on the control stick. Dennis, looking down to the seat next to him, noticed that she had packed a paper bag filled with his favorite sandwiches, ham and cheese wrapped in waxed paper.

As he unwrapped a sandwich and took his first mouthwatering bite, the engine of the magical zeppelin emitted a barely audible *chug, chug* sound as it rose gently into the air and turned silently north. Dennis glanced down and watched the roof of his house recede slowly into the distance until it became a tiny dot. He then craned his neck upward and gazed into the starry expanse stretching out above them.

It is up there somewhere, he thought happily. *An actual island floating in the sky.*

"Mom, how long 'til we get there?"

Betty Avian smiled at his eager expression.

"We have a dinner date at eight tonight with Jasper and Summer. We will be there before then."

Dennis groaned. He had been looking forward to exploring Sof' City, the spongy training city where students could bounce off of fifty-foot-tall skyscrapers and throw inflatable cars at villain targets.

"Aw, Mom. Do we have to? Summer's so, I dunno, grumpy all the time."
The boy stared out the window.
"Couldn't we reschedule?"
"Nope."
Miss Avian banked the airship through a large cumulonimbus cloud.
"Denny . . ."
He noticed that there was a slight hesitation in her voice.
"Yeah?"
"There's something important we need to talk about."

...3

ZANZIBAR'S

A GIGANTIC waiter, clad in a turban and riding an ornately designed magic carpet, floated to an abrupt stop in front of the table. Summer noticed that the waiter's skin was green, and that he wore many ancient-looking jeweled rings on his long fingers.

"Good evening and welcome to Zanzibar's." The genie surveyed the table, and noticed Summer and Dennis who were deliberately avoiding eye contact with each other. He smiled, showing many very white teeth as he addressed Jasper and Betty.

"Have the children ever been here before?"

Summer prickled as she heard the waiter refer to her as a child. Please. Who was he kidding? She was fourteen!

Summer felt Dennis's eyes upon her. As she turned to meet his gaze he quickly glanced up at the ceiling, carefully avoiding eye contact.

He knows, Summer thought.

Dennis was being uncharacteristically quiet, and hadn't even mentioned Captain Truehart one time since they sat down. The unspoken awkwardness about the news of the upcoming marriage was palpable.

Jasper cleared his throat and glanced up at the waiter.

"No, they have never been here before." He gave the kids a lopsided grin. "Maybe you should let them know what they are in for?"

He grinned at the massive genie who responded by giving Jasper a huge wink.

"Very well then." The genie reached into a pocket in his gold-trimmed vest and removed a small oil lamp. With mock seriousness, he flashed Summer and Dennis a conspiratorial grin.

"What you need to do is think of your favorite color." The green giant moved the salt and pepper shakers out of the way and placed the lamp in the center of the table. "Then rub the lamp three times and say it aloud."

He looked around the table expectantly. Jasper, seeing that neither Summer nor Dennis made any motion to take the lamp, offered it to Betty. The pretty brunette gave Jasper a smile. She held it out at arm's length, closed her eyes, rubbed the lamp, and pronounced, "Pink."

The lamp puffed out a tiny burst of pink smoke and rattled dramatically. Instead of responding with interest, Dennis scowled and studied his fingernails. Summer felt embarrassed.

Jasper tried to warm the atmosphere at the chilly table. He took the lamp from Betty with a flourish and grinned broadly at Summer.

"Isn't this fun?"

Summer smiled weakly, then lowering her eyes, studied the magic carpet place mat that hovered a few inches above the table.

Jasper, ignoring her unenthusiastic response, rubbed the lamp and boomed, "Aquamarine!"

The lamp puffed out a puff of smoke, this time blue, and once again rattled in response. Jasper nudged Summer with his elbow and offered her the lamp. Summer shook her head slightly, declining the offer. Jasper and Betty exchanged concerned looks.

"Well, how about you, Dennis? Wanna give it a try?"

Dennis glanced up at Jasper's eager expression. He stared at the lamp for a moment, then lowered his eyes once more.

"Aw c'mon," Jasper encouraged.

Dennis didn't respond.

With a sudden inspiration, Jasper lowered his voice in a secretive manner.

"Hey, you did know that Captain Truehart himself used to come here, didn't you?"

Dennis's eyes flickered with interest.

"And furthermore"—Jasper leaned forward—"he and I used to sit at this very table, and he would sit in the seat you are sitting in right now. Zanzibar's was his favorite place."

Dennis's eyes grew round. He looked up at his mother who nodded seriously.

"He's not kidding. I joined them here more than a few times."

Dennis hesitated a moment, then reached for the lamp. After a while he rubbed it, and with a voice barely above a whisper pronounced his choice.

"White."

The lamp coughed up a white cloud and shook violently, knocking over a bottle of Indian spices. Jasper laughed.

"Wow! That was a good one!"

Dennis gave Jasper a big smile and for a brief moment looked as if he were about to say something, but then he caught Summer's annoyed glare and fell silent. Summer felt a surge of jealousy. White? That wasn't a color! Her dad was being way too indulgent with this little brat.

Betty took the lamp from Dennis and, ignoring Summer's scowl, handed it to her, smiling.

"Come on, Sum. You are the only one left."

Everyone's eyes were on her. Summer noticed that Dennis had a sour expression on his face as if he were looking at a piece of rotting fruit. After a few awkward moments of silence, Summer reached for the lamp and sighed deeply. She didn't feel like doing any of this, but seeing that she wasn't going to get off the hook, she went along with it. Okay fine. The stupid kid said "white." Well then, there was only one thing to do. She grabbed the lamp by the handle and polished it roughly.

"Black."

The lamp didn't move. Summer didn't know why she had done it. Black certainly wasn't her favorite color, but all that she could think of at the time was to make a choice that was as far from Dennis's choice as possible.

Suddenly, without warning, the lamp sputtered and coughed. It began to shudder and vibrate rapidly, its golden finish turning a bright crimson red. A loud hissing sound like a room full of snakes escaped from its spout, then it began to dance manically around the table, knocking the cutlery and empty plates to the floor. The crashing and clattering alerted their waiter who rushed over to the table.

A steaming scream split the air. Everyone at the restaurant shouted and covered their ears. The whistling lamp had turned up on its end and, spout pointing skyward, it belched black smoke at an alarming rate.

The genie shouted and motioned for the other waiters to join him at the table.

The lamp's screaming whistle reached a crescendo and then, suddenly, with a flash of light and a resounding *BOOM!* it stopped. When the smoke cleared, Summer was amazed to see that several gleaming silver platters sat in front of each of them.

The restaurant's patrons exploded with applause. Dennis immediately lifted the cover from his plate and grinned broadly.

"Hey, it's my favorite! A hot fudge sundae!"

It was the most spectacular sundae Summer had ever seen. Mounds of vanilla ice cream dripped with chocolaty hot fudge that melted down the sides of the creamy mountain like rich lava. Summer watched as her dad and Betty revealed their dishes, which contained what had to be some of the most scrumptious-smelling food she had ever encountered. Her dad's plate was filled with delicious sizzling chicken perched atop a bed of fluffy white rice. Betty's contained a small pot of cheese fondue with crispy French bread that was hot from the oven.

Just as Summer was about to lift the silver lid that covered her own plate she heard a noise and glanced up. From the back of the restaurant, two golden doors that were etched with ornate illustrations from *The Arabian Nights* swung open. A figure, diminutive but powerful, strode into the room.

Zanzibar himself, the king of the genies and owner of the restaurant, approached the table. Summer couldn't help but stare. His skin was a deep shade of violet, and he had four arms, each moving independently from the others. Two of the hands were writing down something on a pad of paper, while the other two gestured broadly, as if they were embracing the entire restaurant.

On top of his balding forehead was perched a crown unlike any that she had ever seen. It seemed to float an inch or two above his head, and looked something like a triangular chef's hat, except that it was transparent and covered with giant emeralds.

The king's pudgy face had bushy black eyebrows, a small, curled goatee, and wore a kindly expression.

"By the curved slippers of Mustafa Pez! I haven't seen that happen in ages!"

The king was staring at the table happily. Jasper took one of Zanzibar's outstretched hands and shook it. The king's glittering, intelligent eyes took in everything at the table in a glance.

"So, we have two opposites, eh?" He smiled at Betty, who could see that he referred to Dennis and Summer. She nodded and smiled.

"Looks that way."

One of Zanzibar's hands stroked his beard as he looked at Summer with a piercing stare.

"You have ordered a magical dish. One that usually only we genies eat. It may taste a bit (ahem) unusual for the human palate."

Summer stared down at the covered plate dubiously. The king's expression brightened.

"But, then again, who knows? You might like it!"

The waiters chorused in laughter. Zanzibar chuckled, then held out a pudgy hand for silence.

"Please."

He gestured for Summer to take a bite. She looked at her dad with a pleading expression. He shrugged and smiled.

"You ordered it."

Seeing that there was no way out, she lifted the lid.

A great mound of glittering purple substance oozed across her plate. It shimmered and sparkled, and reminded her a bit of Jell-O, except that it smelled powerfully like . . .

"Roses," she concluded. Well, it could have been a lot worse. At least it looked kind of pretty.

After a moment of deliberation as to whether she should use a fork or a spoon, she took the spoon from her place setting and dug it into the gelatinous mountain. Her ears glowed red as she felt the eyes of the entire restaurant staring at her.

She took a bite. Later when she tried to describe the taste to her friends she could never get it exactly right.

"It was kind of like taking a bite of Nature. But not the best parts, like a sunny day or a fluffy cloud. It was kind of like biting into a thunderstorm." That was the best description she could come up with. The food wasn't unpleasant at first, but immediately after she swallowed it she felt uncomfortable. Her stomach growled loudly and, unbidden, a huge belch escaped her mouth.

She blushed furiously.

"Excuse m—"

But she couldn't finish her apology. The rumbling got louder. It sounded like the engine on a moving truck. Then, suddenly, without warning she felt her hair stand on end. Her scalp prickled painfully.

"Oww!" She closed her eyes tightly and rubbed her aching head. The pain on her scalp flared for a moment and then was suddenly gone. The restaurant had fallen uncomfortably silent. She opened her eyes.

Suddenly the entire place exploded in laughter. Summer couldn't figure out what was going on. She gazed helplessly around her. What was that awful smell? Betty had covered her mouth and was trying to hide her convulsive giggles. Jasper choked on his water. Worst of all, Dennis was pointing at her head and booming with unabated guffaws.

"Um, yes. That *can* sometimes happen." Zanzibar shrugged his shoulders helplessly. "It should wear off in a week or so."

Summer excused herself and, blushing furiously, marched to the bathroom. When she got to the mirror she screamed involuntarily.

Unable to make eye contact with herself in the reflection, she stared down at the marbled porcelain floor and studied it for a long moment. She heard the commotion in the restaurant return to the sound of clinking dishes and happy conversation. Tomorrow was the first day of classes. How in the world could she go when she looked like this?

Her eyes stung with angry tears. It was all that little brat's fault. She felt a small kernel of hatred, like a rusty arrow, lodge in her heart. Forcing herself, she looked back up at her reflection.

She had never liked her hair. She always thought that "mousy brown" was a dull color. But it was far, far better than this . . .

Her hair looked like small, leafy cornstalks and extended about six inches from the top of her head. But where the top of the stalks should have been, there wasn't corn. Instead, hundreds of tiny, blinking eyeballs stared back at her with a horrible, bloodshot gaze. And if that wasn't bad enough . . .

Summer sniffed, then gagged involuntarily.

. . . They smelled like rotten eggs.

. . . 4 OLD FRIENDS

"So, tell me again why you are wearing that ridiculous hat?" Archie Collins, aka "Thunderclap," was perched on the comfy sofa in the corner of Summer's dorm cottage.

"Bad hair day." Summer unconsciously pulled the edge of the bright pink beanie lower on her head. She could feel the eyeball stalks undulating gently underneath the hat. Ugh. Early that morning, she had tried to mask the rotten egg smell by first applying a generous amount of Gothic Girl perfume to the alien stalks, but the smell combination was even worse. She had finally settled on wrapping them up with long sheets of plastic cling wrap and shoving the knit cap on top of the whole mess. It seemed to work. At least she couldn't smell anything, but she had to admit that she did look pretty stupid. The hat looked more like a stretched-out woolly sock, and she had only found it because Clocksprocket had it handy and was using it as a tea cozy.

The Zoom's dorm cottages sat on an interconnecting net of thick tree branches high on top of the tallest tree she had ever seen. When she had first started at the Academy, she had been very afraid of heights, and the thought of sleeping in something so high up in the air used to make her feel queasy. Now she was able to enjoy living in her tidy little home much more, although she still had to remind herself not to look down.

Whirr. Click. "Would Master or Miss prefer chocolate-chip or peanut-butter cookies with their hot chocolate?"

Clocksprocket, Summer's robot, held a tray of freshly baked cookies and two steaming mugs in his metal hands. Technically, the clockwork man had been promoted from working as a servant to a member of the Elite Guard, but because he considered Summer to be the reason for his impossible promotion, he insisted on looking after her.

"Thank you, Clocksprocket." Summer smiled at the shiny brass robot. "But I don't have any time for breakfast, I have to get to the Equipping Stations."

"Speak for yourself," said Thunderclap, who grabbed a handful of chocolate-chip cookies and shoved one into his mouth. "Oooch, hot!" He fanned a gloved hand in front of his burning lips.

The two made their way to the elevator that took them down inside the massive trunk and exited at the base of the tree. At the bottom, a small group of friends were waiting for them.

"There she is!" Beetlebomb, his tiny insect wings fluttering, buzzed over to the pair.

Summer hugged her friends whom she hadn't seen since June. Most of the boys looked like they had grown taller by a couple of inches over the summer, except for Beetlebomb, who looked like he had grown a few inches in his waistline.

"Hey, did you hear the news? I got a job!" He puffed out his chest proudly.

"He can't stop talking about it." The massive boy known as Kibosh rolled his eyes. "You would think he had been awarded a trophy or something." Beetlebomb ignored the insult and proceeded to rattle off his exciting news as the group made their way across campus.

"You are looking at the new assistant baker at Captain Creampuff's. You know how much I have always loved that place." The small, buglike boy rubbed his rotund stomach for emphasis. A long arm stretched over, turned itself into a flyswatter, and swatted at him. Beetlebomb avoided the playful swipe with ease.

"Yeah, B, maybe a little too much." Earthworm had been voted "most elastic" kid at Zoom's Academy and was the stretchiest the school had seen in recent years.

Summer grinned. "That is so cool, B, I'm really glad for you."

"Thanks! Hey, what's with the hat?"

"I already asked." Thunderclap shrugged. "Girls and their hair . . ."

"Yes, you are quite right." Summer heard Hugo, Birthday Boy's familiar, soft, and elegant drawl, behind her. She turned and faced the strange gray boy with the black-and-white-striped birthday hat. He smiled, the corners of his cheeks lifting his usually unhappy countenance.

"Why, just the other day I think that it must have taken Stephanie at least an hour and a half before she was ready to go out."

Summer looked puzzled.

"Hugo's got a girlfriend?" she asked.

"Yeah, you didn't know?" Thunderclap chuckled. "Turns out that he and Stephanie Farnsworth have had a crush on each other since last year." He kicked at a small pebble on the worn path that led to the futuristic classroom buildings.

"The Ruby Avenger?" Summer knew that Stephanie was one of the most popular girls on campus and was surprised that she had taken an interest in someone as unusual as Hugo.

"Yeah, can you beat that?" Thunderclap whispered. "Who would have thought it possible."

Summer enjoyed the conversation with her five friends as they made their way to their classes. She remembered last year when she had struggled so much in all of her Equipping Stations, and wondered if her first day back was going to be any better.

I sure hope so, she thought. Privately, she didn't know what to expect. She had ended the previous year a hero, responsible for saving the school. Since she arrived with her dad yesterday morning, besides a few friendly "hellos," she hadn't encountered much that gave her any indication if she was going to be more popular this year than the last.

As they rounded the corner and entered the crystalline building, nothing could have prepared her for what she saw inside.

. . . 5
DENNIS'S FIRST DAY

THRONGS of students packed the hallway, murmuring loudly and craning their necks to get a look at something that stood in the center of the massive corridor.

"What the—" Thunderclap was jostled to the left by a purple, alien-looking girl in white spandex.

"Sorry," she said in heavily accented English.

"No worries." Thunderclap rubbed his arm as the student elbowed her way past.

"I wonder what's going on."

The six friends looked puzzled.

"C'mon, let's see if we can get through." Kibosh led the way into the tightly packed crowd, his bulky frame acting like a snowplow as the group followed in his wake.

"Yes, it is all true."

In the center of the circle stood Dynamo, the muscle-bound instructor that Summer had encountered when she had first taken the tests that determined what superpower she possessed.

"This has never happened at Zoom's before. We have a student who scored a perfect one hundred percent on every test."

He waved his hands to try to silence the excited crowd. There was someone small standing next to him. Someone wearing a crimson suit with blue boots, someone who looked just like . . .

"Dennis!" Summer gasped.

"Who?" Thunderclap asked.

Summer groaned. *It figures.* She had had such a terrible time when she had arrived at the school. As she had gone through all of the tests she had failed them miserably. Her superpower had turned out to be so rare that it wasn't even on the recording devices! And here was Dennis, a huge grin on his face, having passed every test with flying colors.

"Hey, wow, do you know what that means?" Beetlebomb hovered excitedly next to Summer's ear. "He must be the first one to do that since Captain Truehart!"

There is going to be no stopping him now, Summer thought miserably. He was going to be impossible to live with from this point on.

"I need to go. I don't even know where my first class is," she grumbled.

Thunderclap looked at her. "Your dad didn't tell you? You only go to the Equipping Stations when you first start in the school. After that it is all about going on Adventures."

"What do you mean?" Summer looked surprised.

"C'mon, I'll show you. We'll all go together." Thunderclap had to shout his reply because the mob at that moment had suddenly erupted into an avalanche of applause, probably in response to something Dynamo had said about Dennis.

"Let's go."

The group of friends edged their way through the mob to the other side of the hallway. Summer couldn't get out of there fast enough. If there was one thing she didn't want to happen right now, it was for her future stepbrother to see that she was jealous.

...6 DEPARTURE

To Summer's surprise, they took an elevator to the top of the Equipping Station building and emerged in a 1960s space age–styled room. Summer thought that it looked just like something out of an old show her dad would have on DVD.

The room pulsed with a bizarre purple glow, and a desk full of sliding knobs and flashing amber lights glittered in the corner. There was a platform with seven large transparent capsules standing on the opposite side. Thunderclap moved to the console table.

"Okay, get ready for transport. Everybody take a power pod."

Summer followed the others to the platform and stepped inside one of the transparent chambers. Thunderclap adjusted a few knobs and then turned a large chrome switch. An electrical hum filled the room.

A light flashed, just like when a camera timer is about to go off, and Thunderclap dashed to one of the remaining empty capsules.

"Here it comes!"

The flashing light accelerated and was followed by a sudden burst of radiant light. The next thing Summer knew, her body was covered with a tingling sensation that felt just like when her foot fell asleep. Seconds later she emerged in a part of Zoom's Academy that she had never seen before.

Huge spotlight beams split the sky, and countless launchpads with rocket ships extended into the vast distance. Emerging from the capsule, Summer almost tripped on the steaming hoses that were strewn everywhere.

This reminds me of my dad's basement, she thought abstractedly as she looked skyward. Last year she had been shocked to find that her dad had a secret passage that led from the entertainment center in the living room to down under the house, where he kept a homemade rocket ship. They had taken it all the way up to Zoom's, but had had a close call with the landing. Fortunately, when they made the trip to the floating Academy, her dad had already invented a device that kept the passengers who were afraid of heights in a state of blissful sleep.

Summer and her friends made their way to a platform where a large group of students on the far side of the massive cavern were studying a floating departure board. Summer had seen something like it in an old movie. It had tiled numbers and letters, and flipped to reveal departure and arrival times. As they watched, several of the tiles cascaded down. A pleasant female voice crackled over a loudspeaker.

"Now departing on Platform Seven, all transports to Planet Ziff, with stops at the Horsehead Nebula, Betelgeuse, and Farfarminjin Six. All students departing, please bring your departure pass to the Moon Man and Miss Avian at the gangway. All aboard!"

"Wow, we barely made it." Thunderclap indicated a row of large metal boxes nearby. "Let's hurry and get our passes."

Summer felt herself rushed along to the "Jules Verne"–styled computer station, where after a quick scan of her thumbprint, she was given a light blue slip of paper. The others followed suit, and were soon gathered with the small group at the foot of a shiny, massive ramp that twisted upward to the impossibly high door of the rocket.

Huffing and puffing, they made it to the top and were greeted by her dad, who Summer belatedly remembered had the superhero name "Moon Man," and her future stepmom. As the small group of about twenty students gathered at the top, Summer exchanged a smile and a small wave with Stephanie "The Ruby Avenger" Farnsworth. Hugo picked her out of the crowd as well, and after politely excusing himself made his way over to her side. Betty Avian completed the head count and nodded at Jasper, who smiled and motioned for silence.

"Okay, people, let's settle down." The crowd's murmur quieted into silence.

"Can everyone hear me?" Cries of "no" and "yes" went up from the assembled group. Jasper scanned the small group and decided to proceed.

"For some of you this will be your first off-planet Adventure." He flashed Summer a quick grin. "For others, this will be a bit different from the other destinations we normally go to." Excited murmurs spread through the group.

"We will be going to Planet Ziff. A destination that no Zoom's student or faculty member has traveled to in recent history."

Summer had a flash of recollection at the name. Clocksprocket, her robot, had mentioned something about the planet in a conversation when they first met. She couldn't remember exactly what he had said about it though. She watched her dad with renewed interest.

"Principal Zoom received an important interspatial telegram from our contact on the planet. We have been informed that there has been some kind of unusual storm front that has swept through the settlements up there. The people need help with many of the basics, like rebuilding houses, finding lost loved ones, rescuing kittens up in trees, you know . . ." Moans went up from several students. Jasper quickly motioned again for silence.

"Now, now, not all hero work is glamorous. I'm sure when you get back here to Zoom's there will be some more crime fighting to do down in Megapolis. The villains, no matter how many times we beat them, never give up." Jasper smiled lopsidedly at Betty as Miss Avian stepped to the microphone.

"Please form an orderly line to the left of the ropes and have your departure passes ready. NO PUSHING!"

Summer had a nervous knot in the pit of her stomach as the line inched forward. She hoped desperately that her dad had packed the Hypno-Helmet that had put her to sleep on the ride up from home to Zoom's. Thunderclap was next to her, looking excited, but when he saw Summer's pale expression, he whispered gently, "Hey, you'll be okay. They have special rooms on the ship where you feel like you are standing absolutely still. There are even portholes for people who have motion sickness that have projections of grass and trees and stuff so that you feel like you haven't left Earth. It's like you are just sitting in your living room, looking out the window."

Summer smiled weakly, grateful for Thunderclap's kind words. The news helped a little, but her stomach still flip-flopped awkwardly as she handed the blue pass to her dad and stepped inside the rocket.

The inside didn't look anything like what she expected. She had seen news footage of the space shuttle, and this didn't look remotely like anything NASA would have created. In fact, if she thought about it, it looked more like a cruise ship than a rocket.

The hallways were compact and decorated with a 1960s space motif. Pictures of Saturn, Mars, and various nebulae decorated the walls. Lounge chairs were arranged neatly by a large bay window and various vending machines that sold everything from plastic souvenir rockets to "Super Suit Sewing and Repair Kits" were lined up against the opposite wall. Summer noticed with pleasure that one of the spiral racks in the machines had a capsule labeled *Stargazer's Magic Hair Elixir.* Summer stopped in her tracks. Feeling curious, she put her nose to the glass to read the fine print label. Underneath the picture of a beautiful heroine with flowing black hair the label read:

Tired of villains pulverizing your hair with gelatinous ooze? Did the last death trap you escaped from contain harmful, damaging chemi-

cals? Try Stargazer's Elixir. Guaranteed to bring your hair back to a healthy, SUPER shine.

Summer pulled unconsciously on the awful hat. Fishing in her pocket, she took out five dollars and placed it into the bill slot. The spiral coil spun, releasing the capsule that clunked to the bottom of the machine. Summer reached down and took the container from the metal flap.

"Whatcha got there?" Thunderclap peered over her shoulder. Summer pocketed the small capsule quickly into the utility belt that her dad had made for her last year.

"Nothing." She felt her face blush. Thunderclap looked at her curiously, but wisely held his tongue.

Outside the ship, Betty Avian and Dennis were sitting at the Jetpack Café waiting for Principal Zoom to arrive.

"Aren't you going to eat your doughnut? It's a jelly."

Dennis stared over his mom's shoulder at the tall rocket. "Not hungry. Mom?"

"Yes?"

Dennis poked a plastic fork into the pastry, making it stand on end. "Why doesn't Summer like me?"

Betty's face softened. "Oh, honey, I'm sure she does. She's just having a hard time adjusting to the whole idea about her dad and me getting married."

Dennis scowled. "She hates me. I can tell by the way she looks at me."

Betty moved to the seat next to her son and put an arm around his shoulders. Dennis leaned into her embrace.

"I try to be nice, but it's like, I dunno. I get uncomfortable and say stupid things."

Betty looked thoughtful. "Well, she probably didn't like it when you laughed at her hair at Zanzibar's last night. That might have hurt her feelings."

Dennis couldn't help smiling. "Yeah, but I couldn't help it. It was funny."

Betty allowed herself a small smile. "I know, but girls her age are very sensitive about their hair."

Betty glanced up and noticed that Mr. Fleet was crossing the corridor to pick up Dennis and take him to his classes. "I see Mr. Fleet."

She looked down at her pensive son. "Listen, I'll try to have a talk with her. Everything will work out okay."

Dennis saw the fast-talking running coach stop and talk to a small student who appeared lost.

"Mom, can't I come with you? Pleeeease?" He gazed up at her desperately. Betty smiled and tousled his hair.

"No way, José. You have to go to your Equipping Stations. Next year."

Dennis jabbed at his doughnut, making the jelly squirt out onto his plate. Betty glanced at her watch and kissed her son on the cheek.

"I have to get back inside. You go with Mr. Fleet and do everything he says, okay?"

"Okay." Dennis grumped.

As he watched his mom walk back up the glittering platform, Dennis noticed Beetlebomb fishing through his pockets at the snack bar, gazing hungrily at a large chocolate pastry in the window.

A sudden thought made him smile.

Why not? He grinned and leaped off the chair before Mr. Fleet could see where he had gone.

...7

INTRODUCTIONS

THE students were herded into a very large round stateroom with titanium floors and shimmering tapestries. Miss Avian checked to make sure that the last of the stragglers entered the room, then walked over to a control panel and threw a switch. Sliding panels in the walls opened, and white contoured chairs slid soundlessly out of the walls and locked into place around the room.

"Okay, everyone, please take a seat." Betty's amplified voice echoed in the immense room. With some shuffling and sliding, the twenty students took their seats and looked to Miss Avian expectantly.

"Before we launch, I thought it would be nice to make introductions all around." She smiled prettily at the assembly. "Let's start over here with you, Stephanie. Please introduce yourself using both your real and 'super' names, please."

Stephanie nodded and with a confident toss of her carefully styled hair boomed, "Stephanie Farnsworth. The Ruby Avenger."

Summer noticed that she was wearing her usual red tights with silver belt, cape, and boots. The outfit looked expensive, and probably was. Most people believed the rumors that she came from a wealthy family who were personal friends of Principal Zoom. The next student, a funny-looking boy with curly red hair, jumped from his chair, leaping fifteen feet into the air before making a less than perfect landing, almost crashing into Miss Avian.

"Oops. Sorry, Miss A." The boy recovered his balance and adjusted his goggles, which had slipped down off one eye. The class snickered, and the boy flashed a toothy grin.

"Corban Jowell. Most call me Wonder Frog." He took his seat without jumping, much to everyone's relief.

The next student was someone Summer thought she hadn't seen before. But then, after squinting a bit, she recognized the face. The girl had been a pint-sized pixie the year before, but now had grown significantly. She still had gossamer wings, and when she smiled there was something about her that Summer liked immediately.

"Emilie Joyeux." Her small voice projected loudly in the chamber. "I am still working on a name I like. Last year I was Pixie, but this year I'm thinking of something more like HypnoGirl, now that I've discovered my 'true' powers. But then again, Pink Starlight or maybe Ruby Unicorn would be nice, but I don't want to copy Stephanie or anything, anyway I don't know yet for sure so you can just call me HypnoGirl for now, or Emilie I guess, until I settle on one for sure, but like I said I'm still deciding but I do think that this costume is one I like for, you know, now at least." She blushed and sat down breathlessly. Miss Avian gave a smile.

"Emilie and Stephanie are both Aviation students in my homeroom. Now let's see, who's next?"

She indicated the next student, a tall boy in purple and green who wore a large, shiny helmet.

"Chromedome," he said awkwardly and sat down. Summer tried to stifle a giggle. The boy, suddenly realizing that he had forgotten to say his real name, stood self-consciously and mumbled, "Martin Truehart."

A shocked silence fell on the room. Did Tommy Truehart have a brother she had never heard of? Thunderclap, who was sitting next to her, stared at the boy with his jaw hanging open. Miss Avian, sensing the awkward silence, stood up from her chair.

"Martin is the nephew of the late Captain Truehart and is joining us at Zoom's, having transferred in as a second-year student. He was homeschooled by his mother, who used to teach here at the school." She smiled at the thin boy, who blushed a deep shade of crimson.

"Welcome, Martin."

As she continued down the list, Summer couldn't stop looking at Martin, who looked miserably uncomfortable and slumped self-consciously in his chair. The names continued to rattle off:

"Camille Gloria . . . Glory."

"Alex Chriztof . . . the Engineer."

"Livie Rose . . . Moonbeam."

Summer felt sorry for Martin. She knew from experience what it was like to have a family that had both heroes and villains in it. After all, her own father's brother was head of Graves Academy, the home of the world's worst supervillains.

"Jake Rosenbaum . . . Kibosh."

"Laticia Bryant . . . Shimmer."

"Archie Collins . . . Thunderclap."

Summer was so busy empathizing with Martin that she hadn't noticed it was her turn to introduce herself. Startled by Thunderclap's elbow nudge, her face blushed in embarrassment as she stood up.

"Summer Jones . . . uh . . ." She had often thought about choosing a name for herself but had never been able to come up with one. Everyone called her Summer and she was most comfortable with that. She looked helplessly at Miss Avian for support. She was dimly aware of the assembled crowd whispering excitedly and pointing in her direction. She pulled the corners of the horrible hat a little lower over her ears.

"Most of you know about Summer from last year's victory over the Graves Invasion." The crowd stopped whispering. Summer smiled awkwardly as a few of the students gave her an encouraging thumbs-up sign.

"She is the first Enhancer that the Academy has seen in quite a while. Her rare talents and abilities will be an essential help in many days to come. She also"—Miss Avian's eyes twinkled—"is about to become my stepdaughter." Betty flashed a smile at Summer, who felt very embarrassed. The crowd clapped politely.

Why did she have to mention that? Summer thought as she sat down.

The rest of the roll call continued, introducing many students that Summer had never met before. As the circle moved back to the beginning, to Hugo, "Birthday Boy," who sat next to Stephanie, Summer suddenly realized that someone was missing.

"Where's Beetlebomb?" she whispered to Archie. He looked around the room.

"Isn't he sitting over by Earthworm?"

"No. Earthworm is sitting next to that girl with the really tall hair." She indicated a spot about ten seats to the right where Earthworm sat, mesmerized by a girl with the largest bouffant hairstyle that Summer had ever seen. Thunderclap shrugged.

"That's weird. I thought he was right behind us."

As the room emptied, many people in the group stayed behind to socialize. Summer and Thunderclap were joined by Kibosh and Earthworm and they all left together.

Outside of the room, a robot flight attendant handed each of them the key to their own cabins.

"Please return to your cabins for takeoff. We will launch in T minus two minutes."

"We better go." Thunderclap led the way down the winding corridor to a set of elegant doors down a red, carpeted hallway. The group agreed to meet after takeoff and retreated to their individual quarters.

As Summer walked down the hallway to her room, she caught sight of a student through the opened door of one of the cabins whom she hadn't seen boarding with the rest. He was making unusual music on an unearthly instrument. Feeling surprised, and lucky that she had spotted him, she remembered that she had never gotten a chance to thank him properly for helping her during last year's battle.

She knocked hesitantly on the door. The silent boy with the broad-brimmed hat stopped playing his unusual horn and looked up. He smiled mysteriously as she entered.

"Hi, Snazzoo."

The boy nodded at her.

Summer, feeling shy, blurted out what she had come to say.

"Listen, I never got to say thank you for giving me the 'word' last year. It really helped me, and it helped to save Thunderclap's life."

The masked boy grinned quietly. Then, to Summer's surprise he once again picked up the instrument he had been playing when she walked in. It looked like a twisted horn made of blue clay. Next to it was a pile of sheet music.

The boy put the instrument to his lips and blew a buzzing blast,

a long note like the hum of a didgeridoo. Then he pointed at a pile of sheet music and said to Summer in a whisper, "Clef."

Summer smiled awkwardly. She knew that the Mysterious Snazzoo's superpowers were dependent on him never saying the same word twice. Each word he spoke had special powers, and if he ever spoke to someone else it was to gift them with one of his powerful words. Archie had told her that he did this very rarely, and now it had happened to Summer more than once.

Feeling confused, but thankful nonetheless, she nodded her head, blushing, and exited the room. As she walked briskly to her room she privately wondered what the word meant and when she would need to use it.

Summer unlocked the door to her cabin and gave the room a perfunctory inspection. It looked amazingly like her bedroom back home.

Guess my dad had something to do with that. Knowing that Jasper would have wanted her to be comfortable on the long flight, she noticed that a large wooden crate stood next to the bed. Feeling curious, she walked over to it and opened the lid.

All four sides of the box fell open, revealing a familiar, shiny metal man inside.

"Clocksprocket!"

The robot twiddled his tin mustache happily.

"At your service, madam." He bowed stiffly.

A loudspeaker suddenly crackled overhead. "All students please report to your quarters and secure yourselves immediately. Takeoff is in T minus thirty seconds."

Clocksprocket helped Summer into a comfortable safety harness that stretched over the white, padded recliner in the corner. Her stomach was turning violent somersaults.

Please let nothing go wrong, she prayed silently as she fastened the buckles around her midsection. Clocksprocket walked to the corner of the room and pressed a button on his chest. With a loud *CLANG!* he magnetized himself to the wall.

A new voice came over the speaker. A commanding voice began the familiar countdown.

10 . . .

9 . . .

8 . . .

7 . . . Summer squinched her eyes tightly shut.

6 . . .

5 . . .

4 . . . "Here it comes . . ."

Her heart felt as if it were going to leap right out of her chest.

3 . . .

2 . . .

1 . . .

LIFT OFF!

From somewhere far below, the massive engines ignited. The spaceship shuddered violently for a few moments and then, slowly, ponderously, began to rise through the clouds. Even with her eyes shut, she could feel the room start to spin. *Dad, why didn't you pack that helmet?* she thought desperately as her eyes rolled back and everything began to slowly fade to whitish gray.

. . . 8 THE FINAL FRONTIER

"*T*WEET, *twirp, twirp . . .*" The sound of twittering birds invaded Summer's consciousness. She was suddenly filled with intense relief. She had been dreaming that she was on a massive rocket, hurtling into space. What a relief to find out that she was still safe, on nice solid ground. Had she left her bedroom window open?

"Hey, are you okay?"

The concerned voice spoke from what seemed to Summer a million miles away. She cracked open her eyes, feeling groggy, then quickly shut them when she was hit full in the face by blazing morning sunlight.

"I think you passed out."

Summer reached up to shade her eyes from the sunlight and look around. As she did, she noticed with sudden, dawning horror that she couldn't feel the band of the pink hat she had been wearing! It had somehow fallen off her head! Suddenly, feeling wide awake, she jolted up in the reclining chair.

"Um, if you are looking for your hat, I put it over there on the dresser."

Summer looked at the source of the kindly voice. To her surprise it was one of the girls she had seen earlier in the room where they had made introductions. She had long blond hair and big blue eyes that gave her face a perpetually "surprised" look.

"I hope you don't mind, but I, well, I saw what had been done to your hair, and I fixed it."

She blurted out the last of her sentence in a hurry, as if she hadn't been able to help herself.

Summer raised her hand to the top of her head, and didn't feel the greasy eyeball cornstalks, but the reassuring touch of her own natural hair.

"Wow. Thanks." She blushed.

The girl smiled broadly, obviously pleased. "It was no problem. It is part of my superpowers, actually."

The girl looked at the far wall self-consciously.

"Most people think my powers are kind of stupid, so any chance I can get to use them I do." The girl moved to the drapes and opened them wide.

"Oh, and I thought that maybe the Spring Program would be nice. It makes the trip go so much easier when you can look outside and see the grass and clouds."

Summer looked out the window. The birds she had heard earlier were singing in the branches of a large elm tree. Looking outside of this window felt as if she weren't moving through space at all.

I wish I had thought to turn that program on before takeoff, she thought as she walked over to the small mirror above the dresser to inspect her hair. When she caught sight of her reflection she gasped.

"Do you like it?"

Summer couldn't believe it. Her hair was styled beautifully, and it looked, well, there was no better way to describe it. It was gorgeous.

"How did you? I mean, wow! It's amazing!"

The girl laughed and moved to stand behind Summer at the mirror.

"Thanks. I thought it turned out especially well. Oh, and by the way"—she scowled down at the capsule of *Stargazer's Magic Hair Elixir* that lay on the dresser top—"don't use that stuff, it gives you split ends."

Summer turned and smiled at the girl and offered her hand. "I'm Summer."

The girl shot back a big smile and shook her hand. "I know all about you." Her eyes twinkled merrily. "I'm Denise. Most people know me by my super name, 'The Stylist.'"

As the girls shook hands Summer noticed that a pile of lacy pink luggage had been moved into the large cabin and was piled neatly next to a second bed that had materialized in the room.

"So, I guess we're roommates?"

"Yep, guess so!"

It was a new feeling for Summer to make friends with someone so easily. Back in Thousand Oaks she had really struggled with friendships; most of the girls in her junior high had been really mean and clique-driven, but up here at Zoom's it was a different story. She allowed herself a private smile. If the situation with her family was all "out of whack" at the moment, at least she had some friends that she could talk to. Summer couldn't resist turning and looking at her reflection once more in the mirror.

"Denise?"

"Yeah?"

Summer stared at the beautiful reflection staring back at her. She had never worn much makeup, and the way that Denise had touched up her features was nothing short of miraculous.

"Don't let anyone ever tell you that your powers are 'stupid.' I think they are more amazing than any I've ever seen."

Denise flushed, feeling pleased.

KA-BOOOM!

Suddenly the girls were flung across the room as the rocket lurched sideways from the impact of something huge colliding with the outside of the ship. An alarm, hidden somewhere deep in the bowels of the spacecraft, began a monotonous *whoop, whoop, whooping* noise. Summer was shaking and held on to the side of the dresser for support. The ship vibrated as if it were falling apart!

Outside the portholes, the Spring Program flickered with pulsing static. The birdsong died away suddenly and was replaced by an accurate view of what was really there. It was a view of millions of hurtling stars flashing past the window like silver glitter blasted out of a cannon, punctuated by exceptionally large space rocks. Summer's stomach lurched crazily and she thought she was about to become violently sick.

"Never again. I will never let my dad convince me to ride in one of these stupid things ever again!"

. . . 9
DARK SECRETS

DEEP down under the murkiest depths of the Pacific Ocean, the illuminated windows of Graves Academy glowed with a pulsing, sickly, purple light. Inside one of the algae-covered windows, a figure stared out into the ancient gloom, a figure that wasn't wearing his everyday form.

Bubbles burst open and rushed upward as a chamber door beneath the school opened and two members of the security team wearing black and silver diving gear swam out into the water. They carried a struggling form between them, a member of the faculty that Graves had long suspected was a spy.

"It won't be long now."

The two security guards forced the hapless teacher into shackles on a stone pillar that jutted up from the reef surrounding the school, then hurriedly made their way back inside to the safety of the underground portal, shutting the huge door behind them.

Several bubbles, each containing a suppressed scream, emerged from the traitor's mouth as Graves watched huge, megalithic shapes emerge from the watery shadows. His ancient sharks were very reliable and always hungry.

There was a hesitant knock at the door, followed by a creak.

"Sir, you sent for me?"

A boy of about twelve years of age, wearing a skull-shaped mask and tattered cape, stood at attention by the heavy black door frame. Graves did not turn his attention away from the spectacle below.

"Yes, Skullkey, I want you to tell Mr. Truehart that I have located the ship. We are leaving for Planet Ziff immediately. I want the team assembled and ready for transport in five minutes."

The nervous boy clicked his heels together and saluted. As he turned to go, the commanding voice stopped him short.

"Oh, there is one more thing." Graves's new face, the one that looked remarkably like Jasper Jones, smiled cruelly. "Inform them that the Ziffians have been brought back due to the special 'storm front' that I have generated on the planet surface. Everything is proceeding perfectly according to plan. We should have the Enhancer with us by midnight tomorrow."

The boy gulped and shut the door behind him, not daring to delay in doing his master's bidding.

Graves walked over to an ornate mirror and gazed with distaste at his reflection. If everything went according to plan, he would never have to look at the stupid, silly face of his brother ever again. In fact, once the unwitting hand of Summer Jones destroyed the entire population of heroes, Zoom's Academy would finally cease to exist.

He grinned, looking downward at the now empty manacles that hung lifelessly on the stone pillar far below.

This time it was going to work.

...10 SECRET ADMIRERS?

THE girls, feeling badly shaken, recovered their balance.

"What was . . ."

"Shhhhh!"

Summer recognized her father's voice crackling over the loudspeaker.

"Attention! Would everyone please secure themselves into their seats? We have encountered a bit of, uh, turbulence. An asteroid field, actually. Everything will be alright, but it might be a bit shaky for a while . . . WHOA!"

Summer felt the ship rock once again, this time making all of The Stylist's luggage tumble across the room.

After a few harried minutes, the ship steadied back into a normal flight pattern. The girls breathed a huge sigh of relief.

"I really hate heights," Summer confided. Denise, looking pale-faced, nodded in agreement.

"Me too. I have this friend—you know her, Stephanie?"

"Ruby Avenger Stephanie?"

"Yeah, her. Well, you know, she is always flying, always zipping around up in the sky. She told me once that she was going to teach me how, but I said no way."

Denise shuddered involuntarily.

"I can hardly climb up the buildings in Sof' City without getting nervous."

They both giggled. They were interrupted by a knock at the door. The girls looked up as Thunderclap entered.

"Are you okay, Sum?"

Archie's eyes boggled as he stared, transfixed by Summer's new look.

"Wow. You look really nice . . ."

Summer smiled broadly and introduced The Stylist to Thunderclap. Denise shook his hand and beamed.

"So, you're Summer's boyfriend? I have seen you guys hanging out around Captain Creampuff's." Thunderclap and Summer both blushed deeply.

"I'm not, I mean we're not . . ."

Summer laughed. Boyfriend? She looked at Archie, who had turned a deep shade of crimson and was awkwardly fidgeting with his gloves. She hadn't really thought of them as anything but friends. She caught his eye and they both quickly smiled and looked away.

Archie and Summer? She smiled inwardly. Hmm. The thought was interesting.

Her musing was interrupted by the loudspeaker crackling to life once more.

"This is your captain speaking. The asteroid field is behind us and we have clear conditions all the way to Planet Ziff."

Summer rolled her eyes. She would be surprised if that were true. Her dad seemed to miscalculate things a lot.

"So, sit back and enjoy the rest of the journey. By my expert calculations, we should arrive at nine o'clock tomorrow morning."

There was the muffled sound of Miss Avian's voice in the background.

"Oh, yeah, don't forget that tonight is the Heroes Banquet. Show up in your full costumed regalia. Betty . . . er . . . Miss Avian wants me to remind you that T-shirts and jeans are not allowed. Also, after dinner there will be a special movie. It starts at six-thirty. See you all there."

With a loud *click* the loudspeaker shut off.

A banquet? It sounded fun. Summer couldn't ever remember going to one before. The three chatted amiably for a few minutes before Thunderclap declared that he had to meet Kibosh for a game of Space Shuffleboard. As the girls waved good-bye, Denise turned to Summer and grinned.

"Let's get busy."

Summer appeared confused. "What do you mean?"

Denise smiled mysteriously and winked. "We only have four hours until the banquet. We need to get ready."

. . . 11 THE MYSTERIOUS VOICE

"OKAY, so let's see. I think you now owe me two cases of Dr. Lightwave's Power Punch and a Marvelous Mega Muffin at Creampuff's when we get back." Kibosh gloated as he swung the door open to the cabin that he and Thunderclap shared. Thunderclap grimaced good-naturedly.

"Yeah, well I still think that last one was a lucky shot." Archie tossed his silver helmet with the lightning bolts onto his bunk and rubbed a hand through his tousled hair.

"I mean, banking the puck off two slinkers and scoring fifty points in the antigravity pocket. What are the odds?"

Kibosh grinned. "One in a million for you, but for me"—he puffed out his chest proudly—"I rely on my natural talent. No luck involved."

Thunderclap threw a pillow at the hulking boy who ducked, laughing. There was a *chirrup* sound and Archie looked down at his watch. It was five-thirty.

"Oh, man, I'd better get ready for the banquet."

"Yeah, gotta get all prettied up for your *girlfriend.*" Kibosh gave his friend a sly look.

"What are you talking about?" Thunderclap looked perturbed. "Look, why is everyone saying that Summer and I are . . . you know. We're just friends."

"Uh-huh. Sure." Kibosh sounded like he didn't believe a word that Thunderclap was saying. "Everyone can see it, man. It's like the whole world disappears around you when you are talking to her." Before Thunderclap could respond there was a sudden loud noise, like several firecrackers going off in the cabin next to them, followed by the muffled sound of two voices, laughing.

"What was that?"

"I dunno." Thunderclap stared at the wall. "I thought you said that that kid Martin was the only one in that room?"

Kibosh looked puzzled. "I'm sure of it. I saw the list of cabin assignments. Beetlebomb was supposed to be in there with him, but he didn't make it." Kibosh pressed his ear to the wall, listening intently. After a moment, he hissed for Thunderclap to join him. They listened as one drawling voice, presumably Martin's, spoke to another, higher-pitched voice.

". . . and that's without warming up. Once I really get going you should see the sparks fly."

The other voice laughed.

"That's great! Man, I didn't know that your powers were so different from your uncle's." There was a short pause, then Martin's voice spoke softly.

"You do know the truth about my uncle's powers, don't you?"

"Sure I do. Captain Truehart was the most powerful hero Zoom's ever produced. His powers were off the scale."

The small voice sounded full of confidence. There was a pause before Martin spoke again.

"Nope. He actually had no powers at all."

Kibosh and Thunderclap gave each other a stunned look. The smaller voice responded, sounding skeptical.

"Oh, yeah. Sure. Then how about issue twenty-five of his comic book, when he knocked

the entire gang of 'Kaff-fiends' with one punch clear out of Seattle and landed them on the Canadian border?"

"Oh, I'm not saying that he couldn't do those things. I'm just saying that he had a little help."

"Like what?"

When Martin's voice responded it sounded very mysterious. "His cape."

The smaller voice sounded confused. "His what?"

"His cape. All of his powers were in his cape. That is how he scored one hundred percent on all of the tests when he first came to Zoom's. It had been a family secret for generations."

Thunderclap's mind reeled. Could this be true? Everyone at Zoom's believed that the captain was an example of the highest natural powers a hero could possess. The small voice piped up again.

"What happened to his cape after his defeat?"

There was a long pause. When Martin spoke it was with a touch of sadness.

"Nobody knows. Maybe it was destroyed. But you can bet that if Graves knows the secret of the cape, he is dying to get his hands on it."

Thunderclap knew exactly what that meant. If Graves had that kind of power he could shift the balance between the schools. Zoom's had a hard enough time keeping the villains at bay, and after losing Captain Truehart they had been at a huge disadvantage. Fortunately, Summer's arrival had changed that. Having an Enhancer on their side shifted the balance to Zoom's favor.

His mind drifted to how beautiful Summer had looked in the cabin that afternoon. He liked her. He had liked her from the moment he had met her, but had never had the courage to admit it to her.

What if she only thinks of me as a friend. Or worse . . . Thunderclap's mouth grew dry at the thought of Summer saying the words that every boy hated to hear when they were told by a girl that she wasn't interested. *What if she thinks I'm just . . . sweet.*

Well, even if it wasn't true, he admitted to himself that it sounded good that everyone was talking about the two of them being "boyfriend and girlfriend."

He was suddenly jerked out of his thoughts by the alarm clock on his nightstand going off. It was six! With a start he leaped for his suitcase and tore it open, revealing his fanciest super costume.

He hoped Summer would like it.

. . . 12 THE HEROES BANQUET

THE first thing Summer noticed when she walked through the doors that led into the banquet hall was not the sparkling lights or the amazingly lifelike holograms of Zoom's greatest heroes that greeted the students and showed them the way to their tables. She didn't even notice the blazing blue torches that adorned every table, representing the eternal flame of justice that every hero should uphold.

No, there was only one thing she was intent upon seeing when she walked through the doors and that was the expression on Thunderclap's face when he saw the amazing costume that Denise had created for her.

It was midnight blue with periwinkle trim. Her boots were high and made of the softest suede. The delicate silver belt and matching earrings were the final touch, and perfectly complemented the new hairstyle that took Denise a full three hours to complete. She was stunning, and couldn't help feeling a little bit like Cinderella going to the ball.

She gazed around the immense hall. Table after table was filled with happy students all dressed up in their very best costumes. She noticed Birthday Boy, wearing a new tie and talking in quiet tones to Stephanie, who looked beautiful as always.

"Ahem."

Summer turned and saw Thunderclap standing behind her. His helmet was polished and gleaming and he was not wearing his typical green suit. Instead, he wore a suit of similar design but much more elegant, a silver-gray with black trim. Summer blushed. He looked very handsome.

Thunderclap smiled nervously.

"I thought that maybe we could, um, sit together?"

Why does the room seem suddenly so warm? Summer nodded and took the arm that he offered, and they walked together to a table on the far side of the room. When they arrived, Thunderclap pulled out Summer's chair. She sat down, breathing a sigh of relief that she didn't knock over the water glass with her elbow.

Thunderclap took the seat opposite her. Why had she never noticed him this way before? They had been friends, and she felt like she could talk to him about anything, but now, looking at him sitting across from her she suddenly couldn't think of a thing to say.

A robot waiter appeared and offered them both menus.

"*Whirr. Click.* Might I recommend that Master and Miss have a Flooper-Duper Sizzling Punch to begin?"

Summer's questioning glance was answered by Thunderclap.

"It's a really neat drink. It is made from a special juice that comes from the bingle berry. You'll like it."

Summer's face showed concern. "Um, it doesn't have any alcohol in it, does it?"

Thunderclap chuckled. "No way. The only thing it does is make your feet tickle a little bit. I dunno how they make it."

Summer agreed and Thunderclap ordered two. When the waiter left, they picked up the menus and began to read. Summer noticed with surprise that only one dish was offered.

The Main Course: St. Sopwith's Superlong Spaghetti. Served with a special red sauce and savory garlic bread baked at Creampuff's.

Dessert: Chocolate Champions.

"What is a 'Chocolate Champion'? It sounds good." Summer looked over the top of the menu at Thunderclap.

"They are. Man, they really went all out." Thunderclap grinned appreciatively. "My dad bought some for my mom once for their wedding anniversary. It is the finest chocolate in the world and is made from an ancient recipe that was outlawed in Bavaria in the fifth century."

"Why was it outlawed?"

Thunderclap chuckled. "Well, I guess the king tried some and got so obsessed with it he couldn't sleep or eat or anything else. They say he was about to lose his mind or something, so he ordered the chocolatier executed and burned the recipe."

Summer boggled. "Wow. That must be some chocolate. How did they keep making it if the recipe was destroyed?"

"I dunno." Thunderclap took a drink of water. "I guess he must have made copies of it or something."

A waiter arrived carrying two sparkling silver beakers filled with purple juice. True to its name, Summer noticed that the beverage was sizzling and popping. Thunderclap raised his glass and smiled shyly.

"A toast to the coolest-looking costume I've ever seen. You really look beautiful, Summer."

Summer melted. It was the nicest thing any boy had ever said to her. Blushing furiously she gently clinked glasses with him.

Most people know that the worst possible thing to order on a date is spaghetti. No matter how hard a person tries, it is impossible to eat it neatly. Summer discovered this soon enough, and as much as she tried to cut and twist the wayward noodles, there was no easy way around it. Fortunately, Thunderclap had the answer.

"I almost forgot!" He reached into a pouch on his belt and brought out two odd-looking forks.

"Your dad handed them to me on the way in. He says he calls it the 'Neat Noodler.'"

Summer suppressed a groan. Her dad fancied himself an inventor and was constantly creating gadgets that barely, if ever, worked. She thought back to last year when he had invented a "hydraulic device for regulating the flow of maple syrup over pancakes." It was basically a fork with a weird mechanical syringe attached to it that ended up spraying maple syrup all over the kitchen.

Summer reluctantly took the device from Thunderclap.

"Look, I don't know if we should. My dad gets a little crazy with these things sometimes."

Thunderclap shrugged. "What have we got to lose? I mean, if we don't use it we will probably end up with spaghetti sauce all over us anyway."

Summer grinned. He was right. Maybe it would be fun. Together they grasped the handles of the strange forks and pointed them down at their plates.

Thunderclap looked up at her. "Okay, on the count of three. One, two . . ."

There was a spark, and then the forks began to spin, drawing up the long noodles around the tines. When the bite was perfectly portioned, a small laser beam cut the remaining pasta, dropping it neatly onto the plate. Summer was amazed.

"Wow! It actually works!"

The two laughed and enjoyed finishing the meal, thankful that they were granted much relief from potential embarrassment.

After the delicious meal, the "outlaw" chocolate was brought for dessert. After one bite, Summer knew exactly why. These chocolates made the glands in the back of your mouth spasm with enjoyment as they melted on your tongue. It wasn't chocolate. It was every good thing in the whole world rolled up into a single bite.

Suddenly she felt a tingling sensation on the soles of her feet. It was like tiny fingers tickling. The Flooper-Duper Punch had kicked in. Summer let out a squeal, then began to laugh uncontrollably. Thunderclap must have had the same thing happen and began writhing in his seat, snorting hysterically.

After five minutes of constant laughing, the punch finally wore off and left them both gasping and wiping the tears from their eyes.

"Ladies and gentlemen."

The noisy room settled down. Jasper held a microphone at the front of the room and addressed the assembly.

"I just want to take a moment to explain the dual nature of our trip." He smiled and looked out at the expectant faces.

"This mission is special for two very important reasons. The first"—he held up a finger—"is to help out the settlement on Planet Ziff. But there is a more important reason that we are gathered together."

A hush fell over the room.

"Each of you has been specifically selected for this mission based on your powers and abilities. But there are a specific number of you whose powers complement each other perfectly."

Summer and Thunderclap exchanged glances. From the expression on his face Summer could tell that he had no idea what to expect next. She looked back up at the podium where her father had removed a shiny object from a small velvet pouch.

An excited murmur spread through the assembly. Miss Avian stepped up to the microphone.

"As I read your names please stand and walk to the stage."

She unfolded a sheet of paper and read from it.

"Kibosh, Earthworm, Wonder Frog."

The crowd jostled to watch as the three boys awkwardly got to their feet.

"Shimmer, HypnoGirl, Moonbeam." The three girls who sat at a table together stood up shyly.

"The Stylist, Chromedome, Glory, Hat Trick." Summer noticed that some of the students seemed to know what was happening and were holding their breath expectantly, hoping to be chosen.

"Thunderclap, The Ruby Avenger, Birthday Boy, and Summer."

Summer, not quite knowing why she felt so relieved that she had been called, stood up.

Miss Avian smiled. "The Mysterious Snazzoo."

With a flash and puff of white smoke, a student wearing a broad-brimmed hat and mask materialized on the stage behind Jasper and Miss Avian. They both looked startled, then chuckled. Jasper patted the grinning Snazzoo on the back and then turned back to the assembly, smiling broadly.

"And last, but not least, Beetlebomb."

Everyone clapped.

"Congratulations. You are an official 'Super League.' Get to know everyone in your cadre, for they will be the people you depend on most for many years to come."

A cheer went up from the crowd. Summer had just grasped the meaning. It was like the comic books, a group of heroes banded together to fight villains and protect the innocent. She could hardly believe it.

Archie stood proudly and wore an ecstatic expression.

"Man, I've dreamed of this day since I was a little kid!"

His face beamed. Summer smiled back at him. As long as they were both on the same team she was happy.

As they each received their glittering League badges, Miss Avian suddenly realized that Beetlebomb hadn't shown up. She whispered to Jasper, who went back to the microphone and looked out over the crowd of faces with a searching expression on his face.

"Anybody seen Beetle?"

A mutter went through the crowd. Finally, Earthworm stretched his long neck up to the stage and whispered something to Jasper and Betty. They nodded and, after consulting each other, turned back to the microphone. Jasper spoke.

"In light of the fact that Beetlebomb has not attended the League Making Ceremony, the ancient custom demands that we pick an alternate."

Excited whispers spread through the students whose names hadn't been called. Jasper unfolded a separate piece of paper and was about to read a name when suddenly a shout rang out from the back of the room.

"I'm here in his place."

All of the heads in the assembly turned, dumbstruck, as a small figure that Summer immediately recognized strode to the podium. Confused chatter broke out in the assembly. Dennis lifted his head proudly and grinned.

"My hero name is 'General Good.'"

Summer's eyes widened in shock. Dennis stood in front of her dad and Betty with his jaw set and wearing a flashy crimson and blue suit with golden epaulets. The other students pointed and seemed to take this in good humor, chuckling at the pint-sized hero. His arms were folded as if daring the two adults to pick someone else. Jasper looked uncomfortable and Summer noticed that Betty looked concerned.

She stepped off the stage and began a low and intense discussion with her son that Summer couldn't quite hear. Dennis wore a pleading expression and, judging from the look on his mother's face, was also in very big trouble. Their voices rose as the discussion grew heated.

"You are too young! There is no way I will allow it."

"I am the most powerful hero here, you need me!"

"NO! Absolutely not! You are not even supposed to be here. You need training."

"No I don't, ask Martin!"

Chromedome looked uncomfortable and shook his head as if to say, *Leave me out of it*. Dennis was unfazed and continued his rant.

Jasper stepped from the podium and intervened, chuckling. He put a hand on Dennis's shoulder and grinned down at him.

"Now, Betty. You know as well as I do that the rules state that the student with the highest score on the tests automatically fills the spot."

Dennis, sensing victory, beamed at Jasper. Betty looked doubtful.

"But, Jasp, he hasn't even been to any of the classes."

Jasper patted her arm comfortingly.

"As soon as we get back to the school he can make them up. It isn't like this mission is going to be dangerous or anything."

He playfully tousled Dennis's hair.

"How's that sound, eh, sport?"

Dennis let out a *whoop* of joy and joined the others onstage.

Summer seethed. How dare Dennis think that he could disregard all of the rules and show up here, the little twerp. She had finally reached her boiling point. Before she knew what she was doing she blurted out, "What makes you think you're so special? You're nothing but an arrogant little brat who wants to be Captain Truehart!"

Dennis's face registered hurt and embarrassment. "I *am* special." His eyes stung with tears. "You're just jealous because *you* don't have any idea what having superpowers of your own feels like."

It was the worst thing he could have said at that moment. Unwittingly, the small boy had touched on her biggest insecurity. Summer was dimly aware of Thunderclap trying to hold her back. She was filled with an angry red fury like she had never known before. Her whole body trembled.

Without thinking, she broke free of Archie's hold and shoved Dennis as hard as she could, knocking him off balance. Suddenly it seemed to Summer as if everything were moving in slow motion. She heard shouting as Dennis fell with his arms flailing wildly. Then, as he crashed to the floor, his superpowers kicked in and accidentally fired a bolt of blue energy straight through the side of the spacecraft, blasting a large hole in the wall. The small boy's head hit the titanium floor with a resounding *thud*. Horrified, Summer stared at his small body lying very still on the floor and felt a nauseating wave of guilt.

Chaos broke loose in the banquet hall.

The vacuum in the craft roared as the oxygen was torn from the chamber. Chairs flew everywhere. A chandelier broke loose from the shock and cascaded down, splintering into a million tiny shards of glass. Shouts of alarm spread through the panicked crowd. Sensing the danger, Jasper grabbed the microphone.

"Everyone to their cabins immediately! We need to seal off this room! Exit the hall in an orderly fashion!"

Miss Avian herded the hysterical assembly out the doors while Jasper rushed out of the room. The structure of the ship groaned dangerously and an alarm shrieked loudly.

Suddenly the nose of the immense rocket made a huge downward plunge, sending students in the twisting corridors howling as they slid, clawing to the walls for support.

Summer made her way to her cabin past the struggling arms and legs of the terrified students and strapped herself in. With a sickening feeling in the pit of her stomach, she guiltily knew that it was her loss of temper that had caused the accident. An accident that might have cost Dennis Avian his life.

. . . 13 TO THE RESCUE!

"SIR, I'm getting a blip on my radar. One of the Academy ships is in trouble! It will impact the surface in less than a minute!"

The officer in charge, a diminutive hero named Mysterion, acknowledged the report with a worried scowl. He turned to the hero who manned the radar equipment, a young woman whose hero name was Sonic Scout.

"Keep a close watch. I'm going to see if I can find a way to slow down its descent."

"Aye, sir."

The girl turned her attention back to the holographic radar device that she projected with her outstretched fingers. Mysterion left the room and marched quickly to his private quarters.

Once inside he removed a small silver ring from his mahogany desk and placed it on his finger. It glowed with white light, sensing danger. Mysterion issued a command.

"By the ancient warlords of Karnos, I command thee."

The ring glowed brightly in response.

Mysterion pushed a hidden switch underneath the carved tabletop. Soundlessly, the ceiling above his head slid open, revealing a star-studded expanse. Mysterion closed his eyes and in an instant a smaller, ghostly form of himself stepped from his body and rose through the air, rocketing skyward toward the endangered vessel.

On board the ship, the last of the students scrambled into their respective quarters. Many had volunteered to try to help save the ship, but had been quickly advised that there was no way to step outside of the ship without oxygen helmets. The robotic staff insisted that they would be safest in their cabins.

In the control room of the ship, Jasper held the ship's wheel in his sweaty hands and tried desperately to pull up from their catastrophic plunge. Miss Avian was on the radio, communicating with the outpost on the rapidly enlarging planet below.

"This is Academy ship 00407. Mayday. Mayday!"

Jasper strained at the wheel, his forearms bulging with effort.

"Why did Dennis have to provoke her like that . . ."

Betty wheeled around at Jasper with an angry expression and said icily, "Well, if it wasn't for *your daughter's* constant 'egging him on' it might never have happened!"

Jasper clenched his pipe stem between his teeth and groaned under the effort of pulling back on the control stick.

Gasping, he shouted to Betty.

"It's not responding . . . can't pull the wheel back . . . Get Summer . . . Need enhancement . . ."

Betty wasted no time and rushed from the room to Summer's cabin, dragging the frightened girl to the cockpit.

"Summer, you need to enhance your father's strength so that he can pull the wheel back! Hurry, we have no time to lose!"

Wrestling with the familiar feelings of self-doubt that surfaced in any crisis, and resenting the sight of her future stepmother, Summer was forced to fight down all kinds of negative feelings that were rising up within her. It wasn't easy. She approached Jasper cautiously and laid a hand on his arm.

Concentrating, and trying not to hyperventilate, she tried to fill her mind with images of strong things: locomotives, elephants, semitrucks . . . Dennis.

The thought of her nemesis interrupted her. She was still boiling with anger and couldn't get in touch with her powers. Betty intervened, her voice brusque.

"Come on, honey, CONCENTRATE! THIS IS IMPORTANT!"

Summer's face turned red with anger.

"I AM! Will you just lay off me. GOSH! YOU'RE NOT MY MOTHER!"

Summer regretted saying it as soon as it left her mouth, but she was too angry to do anything about it. Betty's face flashed with momentary hurt and confusion, but she quickly regained a calm composure.

"I know I'm not, and I know that you're upset right now. But now is not the time. Calm yourself down and do what you need to do!"

Her dad had no energy to respond to the squabble, as it took every bit of strength he had just to hang on to the wildly bucking wheel.

Summer grudgingly did as she was told. She approached her dad and put her hand on his arm.

"Bulldozers, rhinos, gorillas . . ."

She couldn't do it. She was too angry!

Summer could see the planet's surface hurtling upward, and could even make out tiny lights flashing, the shells from the outpost's laser cannons, as they fought their deadly foe. She looked back at her dad, the veins popping at his temples.

"Summer, strap yourself into the emergency chair and brace for impact!"

Summer hesitated. Betty shouted.

"GET GOING!"

She did as she was told, and watched with wide eyes. Feelings of powerless shame washed over her as the surface of the planet filled the viewing screen.

Betty scrambled at the controls, searching desperately for a button that would override the steering mechanism.

The surface of the planet was so close now that Summer could make out the towering aliens and the tiny heroes locked in combat. If only she had superpowers of her own, then she might be able to do something! The hairs stood up on her arms and the back of her neck. This was it. She was going to die!

She had just witnessed the domed buildings of the Zoom's outpost rising quickly to fill the screen, when there was a sudden jolt that set her teeth on edge.

The ship slowed.

Shaking, white-faced students locked inside their cabins cheered! Outside the window some of them could make out the dim outline of a heroic form. Mysterion was holding the ship at bay with tremendous effort, his small arms straining to slow the gargantuan machine's hurtling descent.

In a few moments the ship had crash-landed onto the planet's surface, severely damaged but not destroyed. Coughing from the smoke that emerged from the sparking command console, Summer felt her dad and Betty help her through the rubble and out the door.

The students slid down the collapsible metal slides that automatically extended from the emergency exits. Once they were gathered safely together, Mysterion breathlessly herded the group into the safety of the largest of the outpost domes.

Behind them there was a sudden blast of otherworldly sound. Summer looked behind her just in time to see a strange-looking, whirling, wavy disturbance in the air settle on the rocket. Mysterion pulled her to the door forcefully.

"It's a time tornado! Quick, get inside!"

Summer couldn't tear her eyes away as she watched the huge ship shimmer for a moment and then vanish. It looked like the ship had never been there at all.

As the door slammed behind her and she felt herself rushed into the safety of the magically enhanced titanium dome, a single thought echoed in her mind.

Whatever a "time tornado" was, it had taken their ship. The only way back home was gone.

Summer's stomach sank to her knees.

They were trapped!

. . . 14 THE SUPPORT TEAM

*B*RRRZZZT! *Fshhhhooom! BALOOOOOM!* The laser cannons at Zoom's Outpost Number Thirty-six shot sizzling blast after blast into the starry sky. Towering over the stark planetary surface was an army of horrible alien creatures. Their many-tentacled arms undulated grotesquely as they shot their own weapons in retaliation, their bulging eyes of viscous yellow narrowed in hatred.

Somehow the defeated Ziffians, an evil race that had once threatened Earth long ago, had returned from their "permanent" slumber.

Mysterion turned off the magnification screen. Jasper winced at the prospects of battling such creatures.

"How are we set up for forces?"

Mysterion swept his long cape from under him as he sat down, scowling.

"We have lost hundreds, Mr. Jones. At this point we can last maybe three more days. When I asked Zoom to send reinforcements the last thing I expected was for you to arrive with a handful of inexperienced students."

Jasper, noting the icy tone of Mysterion's voice, responded, "Look, Albert, I know that we haven't always gotten along, but I'm willing to set our past conflicts aside so that we can work together to protect this outpost."

Mysterion glanced up, an inscrutable expression on his face. After a moment he sighed. "Yes. Forgive me. You are right."

The diminutive hero opened a desk drawer and passed Jasper an ancient-looking book.

"What's this?"

He looked at the tooled leather cover. It reminded him of the type of design seen on Western saddles.

"As you know, this outpost was set up for archaeological research to uncover more about the early history of Zoom's Academy with special emphasis on the War of the Cryogenic Crusaders. Do you know much about it?"

Jasper knit his brow.

"Only bits and pieces. Wasn't the Academy created in the 1800s when the first Zoom discovered that Earth was going to be invaded by the Ziffians?"

Mysterion nodded.

"Yes, that is partially true. But we have uncovered many more secrets about the formation of the school."

Mysterion's eyes glittered.

"Jasper, we are just beginning to realize how much amazing technology we have lost. There are discoveries under the silver soil of this planet that could eliminate Graves and his villains forever."

Mysterion continued. "With the help of the coordinates given in the book you now hold, we were on the brink of discovering an underground cavern that we believe might house all of the secrets we have been desperately searching for."

He hesitated.

"That was when the first storm hit. Many lives were blinked out of existence before we realized what it truly was."

Mysterion stood up from his desk and pointed to a diagram on the wall.

"It is no ordinary storm. It is a time and space anomaly. For lack of a better term, at this point we are

referring to them as 'time tornadoes.' So far they have touched down here, here, and here."

He indicated pins that were stuck into the map of the planet.

"Wherever they hit, anything within reach of the storm is sucked out of the present and placed somewhere in the past. Anywhere in history!"

Jasper pulled the pipe from his pocket and lit it thoughtfully.

"How did you discover that the people that were lost in the tornado hadn't just evaporated?"

"At first we didn't know. Then we received this . . ."

He held up a very old letter. It was yellowed with age and dated 1805. Mysterion set it down on the edge of his desk so that Jasper could examine it more closely.

"This was sent by Harold 'Mole Man' O'Reilly, a scientist who had been lost in the tornado last week. This morning an archaic rocket delivered that letter. Harold's calculations were incredibly well done; he must have estimated that it would take over two hundred years to reach us in the present time."

Mysterion indicated the leather-bound volume that Jasper held.

"We uncovered that book just before the freak storms hit. It appears to be a journal dating back to the early formation of the Academy. All of the entries are signed by an anonymous writer known only as 'Endless.' Toward the end of the journal it mentions the wars with the Ziffians."

Mysterion looked troubled.

"The entries say that the Ziffians would have been unable to be stopped if it weren't for a machine that was brought with the early Zoom settlers from the past. So far we haven't been able to discover what that device was."

Jasper's mind reeled.

"But I thought that they were defeated. How did the Ziffians return?" But just as he finished the statement he slapped his forehead, knowing the answer.

"Of course. The time tornadoes."

Mysterion nodded.

"That is what we think. Perhaps these are the original Ziffians that our ancestors fought, but brought from the past into our present reality." His face fell. "But this time we aren't equipped to defend ourselves properly."

Jasper scowled.

"This seems to have one of my brother's schemes written all over it."

Mysterion nodded and moved out from behind the desk.

"Quite possibly. Without that ancient technology, I'm afraid that our superpowers are practically useless against these aliens."

Jasper's heart pounded in alarm, but he forced his face to stay calm.

"I will notify the students to prepare themselves. Seeing that the rocket has disappeared and is probably lost in some primordial ooze somewhere, we have no choice but to defend ourselves the best we can."

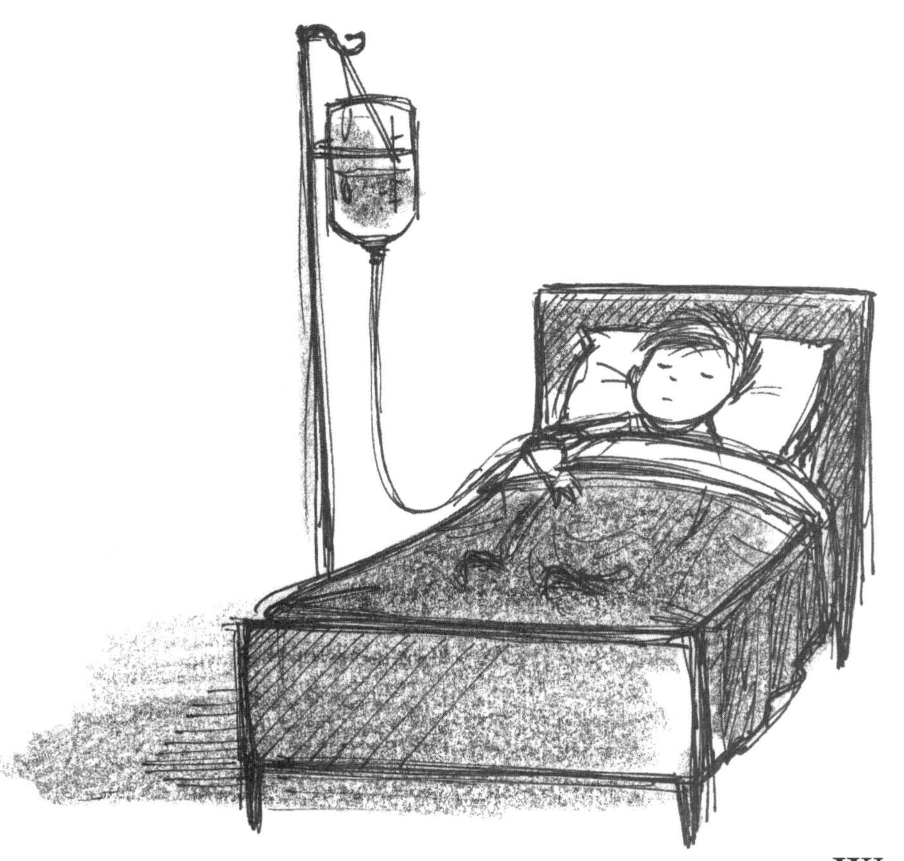

...15 THE HEALING WING

WHEN Betty Avian had informed the doctors at the outpost about Dennis and the "accident" they wasted no time rushing him into the emergency room of the outpost's Healing Wing.

Summer sat on the edge of a small cot in the room that had been assigned to her in the outpost dormitories. She felt terrible for causing the accident and had spent most of the morning alone, sometimes crying quietly into her pillow.

Earlier that morning, she peeked into the room where Dennis lay, white-faced and unresponsive, with his little body tucked gently under the linen sheets. A heart monitor beeped quietly next to him and an IV filled with clear fluid dripped slowly into his arm, keeping him nourished and probably giving him medicine for any of the injuries he had sustained in the crash.

She had apologized to Betty over and over again. She had been so stupid and selfish. Dennis wasn't such a bad little kid, and she realized that her jealousy had gotten way out of control.

Betty had been very nice, telling Summer that it wasn't her fault and that it had been an accident. But Summer knew the truth and hadn't believed her kind words.

Later that day, from a place where she hid around the corner from Dennis's room, she had overheard the doctor telling her dad and Betty the worst of the news. When they checked Dennis's vital statistics they had discovered that something virtually unthinkable had happened. When he had injured his head, he had somehow damaged the part of his brain that gave him his superpowers. They expected him to have a completely normal recovery otherwise, but would always live an existence like any other "mortal" child, with no special powers or abilities.

Summer, feeling heartsick, had watched as Betty buried her face in Jasper's shoulders and sobbed quietly.

There was a knock at the door. "Sum, are you in there?"

She recognized Thunderclap's voice but didn't respond. The door creaked open and he entered. She noticed that he was back in his regular costume, having changed out of the "formals" he had worn at the banquet the night before.

"You okay?"

Summer shrugged and said nothing. Archie sat down next to her.

"I heard about Dennis." He looked down at his shoes. "I know it is really awful, but you can't blame yourself for everything. He slipped."

Summer looked up, her eyes filled with tears.

"But I caused it. I pushed him." She wiped her eyes with the back of her hand.

"I was so mad at him for getting attention, watching my dad being nice to him."

She sniffed and lowered her head again, her hair hanging loosely down next to her wet cheeks. Thunderclap raised a hesitant hand to her shoulders and stroked her back gently. They sat there for a while with Summer crying softly and Archie reassuring her with a silent caress.

"Thanks."

Summer smiled wetly. Thunderclap returned the smile, handing her a Kleenex.

"Have you talked to your dad about it yet?"

Summer shook her head and blew her nose on the tissue he had offered her.

He stood up. "Maybe you should. I was just down in the Inventing Center where he was working on an attack strategy with Mysterion. You should go and see him."

Summer agreed and after a brief hug from Thunderclap agreed to meet him later at the War Room. The word of the unstoppable approaching alien army had already spread throughout the base camp, and if there was one thing she didn't feel up to at the moment it was fighting.

After cleaning up her blotchy face as best as she could in the bathroom mirror, she walked down the hallway, following the signs and directional arrows that led to the Inventing Center.

She had just rounded a corner that led to the room when she bumped into her dad.

"Dad! I was just coming to see you." Summer noticed that her dad didn't wear his customary pleasant expression. His eyes glared down at her and when he spoke, his voice carried an angry edge.

"I was just coming to see you too." He took her arm roughly. "Follow me, we need to talk."

Summer felt hurt and a little bewildered by her dad's behavior. She couldn't remember when he had ever been rough with her before, and he looked angrier than she had ever seen. Her arm was pinched painfully in his grip as she was forced down the hallway and into a side room.

"Sit down," her dad's voice commanded harshly. Summer obediently sat in one of the chairs, her heart beating fast.

"Dad, I'm really sorry about what happened . . ."

"SHUT UP!"

Summer broke off her apology with a startled squeak. Jasper leaned over her with a menacing look in his eyes.

"I don't want to hear your apologies. You have done more damage to our family than I ever thought possible." His eyes glittered coldly as he paced around the room. "I have never said it before, but you have been a constant disappointment to me. Your constant whining and complaining, not to mention your uselessness."

Summer's eyes filled with tears.

"But, Dad . . ."

Jasper interrupted.

"I finally had someone in the family with some real powers. Somebody that I could be really proud of, and you had to go and *mess* it up."

Summer couldn't believe this was happening. Seeing her dad like this was worse than anything she could have ever imagined. Feeling like her heart was breaking, and with tears coursing down her cheeks she reached out a placating hand.

"Daddy. I'm sorry . . ."

Jasper batted her hand away and sneered.

"Yes you are. Very 'sorry' indeed."

He paused dramatically, then delivered a crushing blow.

"I only wish that it had been you instead of him."

Summer's face crumbled to ruin. She stood up from her chair with her chest heaving and rushed out the door, running blindly down the hallway. Nothing her father had ever said to her had hurt so much.

The face of Jasper Jones smiled cruelly. Everything was going perfectly according to plan. Suddenly the smile vanished as he heard muffled voices coming down the hallway. With a flick of his fingers, Graves caused his form to melt, morphing smaller and smaller, finally turning itself into a tiny cockroach that scuttled up the wall and out of an open window.

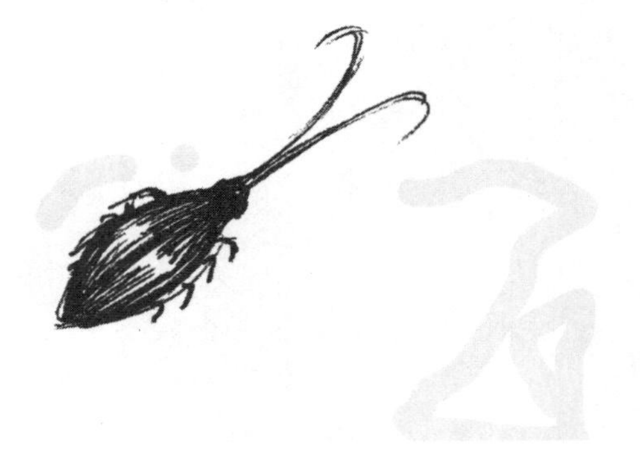

. . . 16 THE WAR ROOM

STUDENTS, instructors, and the remaining settlers on the planet gathered in an immense indoor stadium, the emergency gathering place for War Councils. The crowd hummed with nervous conversation. The myriad of colorful costumed heroes stretched across the benches.

Thunderclap, sitting next to Kibosh and Earthworm, drummed his fingers on his knee nervously and periodically glanced around over the heads of his companions.

"Will you stop fidgeting? You're making me nervous." Kibosh shifted uncomfortably in his seat.

"Sorry." Thunderclap exhaled. "Where is she? She should have been here by now."

Earthworm offered Archie a lopsided grin.

"She'll be here. You can't last five minutes without seeing her?"

Thunderclap smiled back nervously. Something felt wrong. He couldn't explain it, but about ten minutes ago the feeling had started in the pit of his stomach and didn't go away. He glanced up at the illuminated entrance doors.

"Ladies and gentlemen."

The lights in the stadium dimmed as Mysterion, his outline softly shimmering with a pale silvery light, spoke into the amplifier. Thunderclap turned his attention reluctantly back to the stage below.

"I want to start by extending a special welcome to the student delegation from the Academy. Moon Man and Miss Avian have told me about this unique group of young heroes, a number of whom have already participated in a League Making Ceremony."

Polite applause echoed around the room.

"I apologize for the gravity of the mission that you have unwittingly become subject to. When I had last communicated with Principal Zoom the situation hadn't escalated to its current crisis. Your powers will be of much use and appreciation in the forthcoming battle we are about to fight."

The stadium was filled with whispered, concerned voices. Mysterion continued.

"As many of you have undoubtedly heard, we have been invaded by an ancient foe that we had believed to have defeated."

A large holographic image was suddenly projected into the air above the crowd. Many gasped in horror as they witnessed the grotesque form of the alien Ziffians for the first time.

"Outpost Number Thirty-six was set up over one hundred years ago by the Academy shortly after their victory over the Ziffian army. As most of you remember from your Superheroes in History classes, the Cryogenic Crusaders and the Elite Guard were largely responsible for their ultimate defeat."

Many students nodded in recognition of the events, but a few wore confused expressions on their faces, hearing the information for the first time. The terrible monstrous form blurred and was replaced by a new image. This time the image of the Planet Ziff glowed into existence. Thunderclap noted how beautiful the ebony mountains looked placed against the unusual silvery soil of the planet's surface. The rounded buildings of the outpost, looking much newer than they looked today, glimmered peacefully at the foot of a set of sloping hills.

"This image was taken twenty years ago, before we started getting unusual weather disturbances on the planet."

The image blurred again and a new hologram, the same location but with fiercely whipping sandstorms, filled the air.

"The storms were infrequent, but unusually charged with a particle that until recently our scientists hadn't identified. This newly discovered particle was especially corrosive, often causing great sections of buildings to disappear. We didn't fully appreciate its nature until very recently."

A projection of a whirling time tornado suddenly appeared. Many of the students recognized it as the same thing that had descended on the rocket yesterday.

Mysterion went on to describe the anomaly as he did previously to Jasper, warning the students not to get too close if they should see one.

The strategy was simple. They were hopelessly outnumbered and overpowered. The only thing they could do was to try to protect the archaeological dig that was feverishly working night and day to discover the exact location of the cavern that contained the

secret technology, and that hopefully held a weapon they could use to defeat the Ziffians once more.

Miss Avian led the stadium in the ancient battle chant, the one that every Zoom's student or alumni shouted before going into battle.

"We are the heroes of Zoom's Academy!"

The crowd echoed the chant with a roar.

"DEFENDERS OF THE WEAK!"

Thunderclap found himself shouting the familiar words.

"THE STRONG ARM OF JUSTICE!"

The entire stadium rang with the unified shouts.

"THE MIGHTY BASTION OF ALL WHO CALL IN THE TIME OF THEIR GREATEST NEED!"

The crowd was on its feet, the applause echoing through the room like a torrential downpour.

As they were dismissed to gather together at their battle stations, Jasper rounded up the new League that had been formed in the banquet hall for a conference. After a quick head count, he looked around apparently confused.

"Where's Summer?"

The group exchanged baffled glances. Nobody knew where she had gone.

. . . 17 UNCLE GRAVES

SUMMER woke, bruised and battered with her head aching and spinning like she had woken up with the flu. As she lifted her head painfully and looked around, she couldn't figure out where she was.

Towering, slimy stone walls stretched high above her, dripping with moisture. When she tried to move her arms, she noticed with groggy dismay that they were chained to some kind of etched stone pillar, a rugged artifact that was covered with wicked-looking runes and symbols. There were no windows, but the room was lit strangely by a viscous, purplish glow that allowed her to make out most of her surroundings.

The last thing that she could remember was running down the hallway and exiting the building. When she had stepped outside the door, she had heard a shout and before she could turn around something heavy had hit her on the back of the head and everything had gone black.

The memory of the conversation with her father suddenly rushed back into clarity. Her heart ached with a sick emptiness as she remembered the cruel things he had said to her.

Maybe it hurts because he was right, she thought miserably. Deep in her heart, ever since her parents' divorce a long time ago, she had unconsciously struggled with insecurity over her place in her father's heart. She'd always privately worried that the split had somehow been her own fault, that maybe there was something wrong with her, something that had made her parents' marriage intolerable.

I guess that must be true. You always knew it, and now you have finally heard it for yourself. Your dad never really wanted you; you have been nothing but a big pain as long as you have been around.

She felt tears seep into her red-rimmed eyes. She wondered how she could keep on crying when each time she did, her body hurt so badly that it felt like she couldn't cry anymore.

The heavy, rusted steel door that led into her chamber swung slowly open. Summer didn't look, not caring who it was. Several villains, The Blue Ox, Overtime, Lucifina, and Tommy Truehart, entered the room followed by their headmaster, Graves himself.

"Students, let me reacquaint you with my darling niece, the great Summer Jones." Graves moved over to the stone pillar and lifted Summer's chin. Summer avoided his gaze, looking instead down at the moldy flagstones.

"Now, now." Graves clucked mildly. "Is that any way to greet your favorite uncle?"

Summer didn't respond. Lucifina cackled with glee.

"Master! Let me be the first to activate the stone, can I? Can I?"

Graves turned to Lucifina and gave her an indulgent smile. "We must wait to see what Summer decides."

Lucifina scowled with obvious displeasure. Graves folded his arms, staring down at his listless niece.

"I am going to offer you a choice, my dear, and I am only going to offer it *once*."

Graves put his iron gloves behind his back and rocked back upon his heels.

"We are family. Like it or not, it is the sad truth."

Graves proceeded, speaking with obvious relish.

"Your father and I have not gotten along in a while, it is true. But you are part of the bloodline. You have the right to inherit the proper legacy to which you were born."

He turned to face her.

"I am offering a chance for you to join me. With the use of your Enhancement Powers we could rule the world together. I see you as an individual with tremendous potential."

His voice softened to a purr.

"And I will allow you, as my niece, to be second in command. Infinite power at your fingertips, accountable to no one but myself. Think about it."

Summer's head hurt as she listened to her uncle's words. Normally, even the thought of considering a proposal like this would have been unthinkable. But now . . .

Maybe this is where I belong. It's not like I have anywhere to go back to. Even the thought of returning to Zoom's made her feel nauseous. Was there any reason to ever go back?

Her uncle saw the conflict raging in Summer's tired eyes.

"I will give you some time to think about it. An hour should be enough." He turned to Tommy Truehart."

"Mr. Truehart, I want you to answer any questions she might have and help her to see the potential of working with us." A scowl crossed Tommy's face as he looked grimly back at his master. Graves stared quizzically at the handsome youth, his voice taking on a dangerous tone.

"A problem, Mr. Truehart?"

Tommy looked as if he wanted to say something, then thought better of it. He shook his head quietly "no."

Graves smiled. "I didn't think so."

He snapped his fingers and the other students obediently followed their evil master out of the chamber. Tommy waited until the sound of their footsteps disappeared, then exhaled slowly.

"Jerk."

He walked over to Summer and tested the manacles that held her in place. Summer was only dimly aware of what he was doing. The boy concentrated, then placing his fists on the handcuffs, pulled with superhuman strength. As the manacles dropped from her wrists Summer slumped to the ground, her hands tingling painfully.

After a furtive look at the door, Tommy crouched down next to her, his voice low. "Are you okay?"

Summer noticed that his voice sounded concerned. It was a mockery, him talking to her like this after he used her last year to help him break into the Weakness Vault at Zoom's. He made her think that she was special and then turned around and dumped her. She didn't answer him.

"Listen. I'm going to help you get out of here but we have to hurry."

Summer looked up at him with her eyes vacant and hopeless.

"I don't care. Leave me alone."

"I know what you are probably thinking, and you are right." Tommy looked at her with a pained expression. "I shouldn't have done it. It was stupid. I had no idea what I was getting into."

Summer realized that his face had a haunted expression on it, a look of desperation and fear that she had never seen before. She listened.

"I was sick of the comparisons, sick of having to try to live up to my dad's legacy. All I knew was that I wanted it to stop. I wanted people to see me for who I was, instead of just 'Captain Truehart's son.' " He hung his head.

"Like you, Graves promised me that I could be second in command. He played into every emotion I felt about my dad. He convinced me to join him and I did terrible things. Including being really mean and unfair to you."

He looked back down at Summer.

"I know it might not undo the awful things I've done, but I owe you an apology. I . . . I'm really sorry."

Summer glanced up at him. The look of contrition was genuine. But then again, she had believed him once before.

"Why should I believe you?"

Tommy sighed.

"You are right. I don't deserve your trust. But let me tell you something important. It wasn't your dad that you were talking to back at the outpost a little while ago."

Summer's head reeled. How could he know about that?

"What?"

Tommy lowered his voice to a whisper. "It was your uncle. He disguised himself as your dad in order to get you to join his side." Tommy's face showed disgust. "It was a horrible thing to do."

Summer's heart leaped. She hardly dared believe his words. Could what he said be true? She had forgotten about Graves's shape-changing abilities. Last year he had transformed Tommy to look exactly like her when he robbed the vault at the school, an act that had almost gotten her expelled.

She studied his face, looking for a lie.

"It's the truth, I swear it."

Relief washed over her. Suddenly it made sense. Why had she chosen to believe that her dad would have ever said such things to her, when he had always said only encouraging words as long as she could remember? Once again, her eyes burned with tears, only this time they were from pure relief. Tommy smiled.

"If you wouldn't have used your powers for him willingly, he was going to use that thing to suck them out of you." Tommy indicated the evil pillar with a scowl. Summer glanced at it with horror. She was certain that whatever power operated the stone was wicked and most certainly painful. She looked back at Tommy with a renewed sense of urgency.

"How can we get out of here?"

Tommy's face clouded. He suddenly looked very sad.

"I can never leave. When they get you in here and make you a villain he makes it so that if you ever turn traitor you are instantly put to death."

Summer shuddered. "But what if he finds out that you helped me escape?"

Tommy shrugged. "I'm sure that it won't be good."

Summer watched his face, a face that looked so much like his father's right now that it was uncanny. It was a face that had decided once more to act like a hero.

"It is just the chance I have to take." He looked at Summer, his face full of determination. "Come on. I've got a plan."

. . . 18

THE BATTLE-FRONT

A DIFFERENT set of storm clouds, clouds that weren't usually present on Planet Ziff, gathered above Thunderclap's head.

"Good thing it's Thursday," he mumbled and closed his eyes, expecting the familiar, uncomfortable electric shock. Suddenly with a loud *KRACKATHOOOM!* a bolt of blue lightning shot down out of the storm clouds and struck him on the helmet.

"WHAAAAAHOOOOOOOO!" His voice faded into the distance as quickly as a bullet being shot from a gun. The landscape blurred beneath him as he rushed toward the towering alien foe, dragging a long titanium cable behind him.

In an instant he was upon them. He caught a flashing glimpse of long fangs and bulging yellow eyes.

Time for the rodeo!

In a flash, he made a wide circle around the tentacle legs of the closest alien. It was a very wide arc, the gigantic alien was much bigger than he ever thought possible.

Just a little more . . .

He had just rounded the final turn when the unthinkable happened. Suddenly one of the tentacle legs flashed out, quicker than a blink, and snatched him up in the air!

Thunderclap was stunned. They shouldn't have been able to see him when he was moving that fast! The crushing grip of the alien began to close and he howled with pain.

Jasper was watching from the battle line, an optical magnifier of his own invention perched over one eye.

"They got Archie! Move out! Attack formation, NOW!"

Betty Avian soared up into the star-spangled sky, her group of flying students in close formation behind her. They each carried heavy laser rocket launchers that inhibited their ability for the higher elevations, but were the only weapons that they could use to accomplish their goal.

In moments they were within range of the alien creatures. Miss Avian signaled and the group fired, their guns blazing, aiming for the large bulbous eyes of the alien beasts.

One of the blasts, fired by The Ruby Avenger, caught its target. With an explosion, the eye blasted into a million dripping blobs and hit the ground with a sizzle like frying bacon.

"Great shot, Steph!"

HypnoGirl flew beside her, giving her the thumbs-up sign, then shot away, her wings flapping, and hovered dangerously in front of one of the aliens.

"You are getting sleeeeeepy!"

HypoGirl's eyes turned into crazily spinning spirals, and her sparkling pink cape glittered behind her, flashing into the eyes of the nearest alien. It hesitated a moment, then suddenly its eyes transformed, becoming spinning circles as Emilie intended.

It looked like the trance was working, and Emilie was about to speak a command, when suddenly the alien's eyes faded back into their familiar yellow. With a sudden shriek, it retaliated by firing laser beams at the shocked HypnoGirl, who absorbed the full brunt of the blast and tumbled from the sky.

"NOO!" Stephanie shouted as she raced toward the ground to rescue her friend.

Suddenly, out of nowhere, the alien whose eye she had damaged whipped a tentacle in her direction, snatching her out of her midair descent. Stephanie screamed as she felt the air being forced from her lungs.

"Time to put the KIBOSH on this guy!"

From below, the hulking boy raised a huge fist and smashed down on one of the alien's tentacles. With an angry shout, the creature loosened his grip and dropped the unconscious Stephanie, who cascaded to the ground like a rag doll.

Kibosh caught her easily, and setting her and HypnoGirl down in a safe place, rushed over to the aid of Thunderclap.

The battle raged with the heroes taking the worst of it. After about an hour, Jasper sounded a roaring alarm that signified a retreat. Amid massive explosions and enemy fire, the bruised and battered heroes returned to the safety of the outpost walls to regroup.

Once inside, Thunderclap, who nursed a broken arm and was covered with ugly-looking scrapes, moaned.

"Man, these guys are tough."

HypnoGirl leaned weakly against a back wall next to her friend, Glory, who lay on a cot, unconscious. She looked pale and shaken.

"Anybody seen Earthworm?" Kibosh, his breath coming in ragged, heavy gasps, inquired.

Birthday Boy shook his head sadly, and then put a hand on Kibosh's shoulder.

"There is bad news. He was absorbed by one of the time tornadoes."

Kibosh and Thunderclap looked stricken.

Jasper walked into the emergency room where a tired and windswept Betty Avian hovered over her son's bed. Many of the students and defenders were being treated for major wounds, and the room was much fuller than when they had arrived.

Dennis had regained consciousness that morning, but hadn't spoken much since he heard the unfortunate news about the disappearance of his superpowers.

Jasper put his arm around Betty and leaned over Dennis and smiled.

"Hi, little guy. How are you?"

Dennis shrugged imperceptibly. Betty turned her attention to Jasper.

"What is the latest?"

Jasper looked pale and concerned. "I can't find her anywhere. I'm really worried."

Betty laid a hand on his. "She was feeling really guilty, Jasp. I hope she didn't run away."

Jasper looked agitated and ran a hand through his thinning hair. "Me too." He placed his trademark hat upon his head and walked to the door.

"I'm going to keep searching. We need her now more than ever."

Betty stopped him before he exited. "Jasp, how much time have we got?"

He stopped midway through the door and stared at her, looking troubled.

"I don't know for sure. Maybe three hours, maybe less. They are already working on breaching the structure with their lasers."

His fists tightened with frustration.

"They knocked out our communications. There is no way to get help from the school. Unless the miners can find a way to enter that chamber soon and we find out if there is something in there we can use, I'm afraid . . ."

Betty knew the answer. The news had come about an hour ago that although the digging crew had been able to locate the chamber, they had encountered a heavy, ancient, impenetrable metal, which surrounded it. There were no apparent doors, and even Kibosh with his enormous strength had been unable to dent it. Dennis turned over and looked meaningfully at his mother.

"If Captain Truehart were here he could have broken into that chamber, and we would all be okay."

Betty smiled wetly and stroked her little boy's hair.

"I wish he were here too, honey. I really do."

. . . 19 THE CRIMSON CAPE

SUMMER and Tommy had traveled through countless dank and winding corridors underneath the floors of Graves Academy. She had had to step sideways several times to avoid stepping on any of the vile rats that scurried across the wet floor.

"This is it." Tommy's voice floated back out of the darkness.

Summer crouched behind him, listening.

"Where are we?" she hissed.

"It is a secret passage that leads to the alcove above the auditorium. It is where Graves hung my dad's cape."

Summer gasped.

"So, you know the secret?" Tommy's voice sounded flat.

"Yes. Thunderclap overheard your cousin Martin talking about it."

Summer heard Tommy turn.

"Martin is at the school?"

"Yeah, he just started this year."

Tommy let out a low chuckle and spoke softly, "I can't believe it. Marty is at Zoom's."

Tommy's voice took on a wistful tone. "Do you know Wonder Frog?"

Summer thought of the curly-haired boy with the bulbous goggles. "Yes. He is in my new League."

Tommy was impressed.

"You are in a League? Man, that is really cool. Most don't get to join one until after graduation."

Summer blushed at the compliment.

"Well, it's not like we have really gotten a chance to do much together yet. I hardly know everybody in it."

Tommy was quiet for a moment. When he spoke, it was very softly and hesitantly.

"Um, Summer. When you get back to Zoom's, could you do me a really big favor?"

Summer hesitated, then agreed.

"Okay."

Tommy continued. "Would you tell everybody that I'm really sorry for what I did. I . . ." His voice choked. Summer placed her hand on his shoulder.

"Tommy, everybody deserves a second chance."

Tommy sniffed loudly and cleared his throat. They stayed silent for a moment.

"I hope I can have one someday. Thanks, Summer."

He embraced her quickly. Then, regaining his composure, grasped the handle of the door to the passage.

"There shouldn't be anybody in the auditorium at this time of day, but we can't make any noise. Your uncle has detectors and cameras all over the place and the slightest sound will activate the alarm."

Summer nodded in the darkness, and then remembering that Tommy couldn't see her she said, "Got it."

"Good. I am going to get the cape for you, you put it on and then fly as fast as you can at the ceiling."

Summer envisioned crashing on the hard stone roof.

"Won't that hurt?"

Tommy chuckled. "Are you kidding? When you have that thing on you will be practically invincible."

Summer couldn't imagine what it would feel like to burst through a wall of solid rock. The thought of it made her stomach turn uncomfortably. *What if it doesn't work?*

"Here." Tommy handed her something in the darkness. It felt like a small metal skull.

"What is it?"

"It is a tracking beacon. It will help guide you up to Planet Ziff. Once you leave the bottom of the ocean just watch the beacon. It will tell you when you are getting close."

Summer panicked. "The ocean! But I can't swim, how will I hold my breath that long, I . . ."

Tommy hushed her. "Listen to what I'm saying. The cape will take care of everything. Trust me."

Summer never thought that she would have ever trusted those words again coming from Tommy, but she found that this time she did. Tommy grasped the handle of the door and, holding a finger to his mouth indicating that Summer should remember to be quiet, opened it carefully.

They were on a balcony high above a massive auditorium floor. Looking down from the velvet-curtained alcove, Summer could see Truehart's crimson cape hanging directly below them.

Tommy leaned far out over the balcony and tugged at the cape. Summer noticed a confused expression cross his face. He reached down and tugged forcefully, his superpowered arms straining with the effort. Finally, after this didn't work, he motioned for Summer to stand back. With a sound like a pilot light being turned on in an old oven, Tommy's hand burst into flame. Summer watched as he pointed a finger at the cape and shot a blue, fiery line directly at it.

It flared brightly, like a blowtorch hitting steel, then faded. Tommy once again leaned over and pulled until the veins stood out on his neck. The cape wouldn't budge. He motioned to Summer to come closer and whispered into her ear.

"It is bound with an invisible lock. I can't get it."

There was a sound at the far end of the chamber. Tommy, wide-eyed, motioned for them to duck down. Summer listened, her heart pounding wildly, as someone opened the door to the auditorium.

Soft, sneaking footsteps crept down the narrow space between the chairs. Summer found a tiny hole that she could look through and spotted a small boy wearing a skull-faced mask, limping up to the platform on the stage. Looking around furtively, he proceeded to push a hidden lever beneath the wooden pulpit. With an almost indistinguishable shuffling sound it moved over a few inches to expose a narrow stairway beneath.

Tommy exhaled in quiet surprise, his attention on the stairway. When the boy disappeared from view, he leaned back with a relieved expression. He turned to Summer and with sign language indicated his idea for a new plan. She would enhance his powers and he would try again. Nodding, Summer placed her hand on his shoulder and concentrated.

Tommy's muscles bulged and rippled with titan strength as he tried once more to force the invisible lock. To Summer it seemed like nothing should have been able to withstand that kind of supernatural force. But after a few more straining efforts, Summer's heart sank as Tommy collapsed backward, exhausted.

A loud noise suddenly split the air. Up from beneath the platform, the skull-faced boy returned, screaming. He leaped up through the opening, his costume in tatters, and forced the podium back into place. The hair on the back of Summer's neck stood on end as a low, thrumming noise split the air.

"The alarm!" Tommy didn't bother to hide the sound of his voice. He stood up and started to rush them both to the balcony door. Summer was trying to place the sound of the alarm. It was familiar. It sounded just like . . .

"A didgeridoo."

Tommy stopped in his tracks.

"What?"

Summer's eyes grew excited. She had remembered the word that the Mysterious Snazzoo had given her back on board the rocket. Turning back to the balcony she stood over it and proclaimed, "Clef."

At first she thought that maybe she had said it wrong. Nothing seemed to have happened, then she noticed that something small was cupped inside of her hand. When she opened it, she saw the strangest little silver key that she had ever encountered.

"Here, try this!"

She handed the key to the bewildered Tommy, who wasted no time reaching over the balcony and feeling around for the invisible keyhole. There was a small *click*, and the sound of something heavy falling. Tommy stood back up, grinning broadly, the long elegant folds of the crimson cape in his hands.

Below them the doors burst open. Graves, surrounded by a horde of villains, spotted them immediately.

"There they are!"

With a roar the villains swarmed into the cavernous room. Tommy turned to Summer and handed her the cape.

"Quick, put it on!"

"But . . ."

He turned back to her, a fierce light in his eyes.

"I have waited a long time for this . . . Go!"

Summer gave him a quick hug and clasped the cape to her shoulders. Overtime, the evil speedster, burst through the balcony door. Tommy, his face alight with the joy of battle, flew at the boy with his fists outstretched.

As soon as she donned the cape, she felt a tremendous, coursing power fill her body. She had no doubt whatsoever that she could fly, and not only that, she was confident that no wall could hold her back.

Like a bolt of lightning she shot up to the ceiling, blasting through the chamber roof with a shuttering *BOOM!* and into the sea above. Tons of water rushed below her, flooding the auditorium and occupying the panicked villains while she made her escape.

As she shot through the water like a supercharged torpedo, one thought filled her mind.

Having superpowers is the most exhilarating feeling in the whole world!

...20

SAVING THE DAY

JASPER wiped the sweat from his face as he tried once again to pound open the mysterious metal that surrounded the secret cavern. After a few moments, he lowered the jackhammer that he had jury-rigged with a high-powered hydraulic attachment. His arms burned with the effort. He didn't care. He didn't want to think. His heart pounded with the fear that only a parent can know when they can't find their child.

Brratttattatattt! He pushed the machine once more against the impenetrable wall. His mind raced with fear. What if those horrible monsters had gotten her? How could he ever live with that?

His eyes burned with sweat and tears. Everyone else had given up on the chamber, thinking it was impossibly sealed. He felt helpless, powerless to protect his daughter. Angry, he pushed his shaking arms harder against the handles of the machine, forcing it against the wall. Finally, with a burst of rage, he threw the convulsing machine as hard as he could to the ground. As he did, a quiet voice spoke from behind him.

"Daddy, throwing it on the ground isn't going to help."

Jasper turned, unable to contain the sudden joy and relief that flooded his veins like ice water as he beheld his daughter's beaming face. As he held his arms out wide and knelt down, he was filled with sudden memories of Summer at three years old toddling into his arms.

"I'm so glad you're back! I don't know what I would have done if something had happened to you."

Summer buried her head in his shoulder and smiled happily. After a tight squeeze, Jasper set her down. His eyes suddenly widened, noticing for the first time the cape that she wore.

"How 'bout you let me have a try at that wall?"

. . . 21 THE LAST STAND

THE last stand of the Zoom's heroes was going to take place inside of Outpost Number Thirty-six's War Room. The heroes stood, their faces pale and grim, looking up at the massive, domed ceiling, waiting for the Ziffian lasers to break through.

"I looked everywhere," Thunderclap mumbled to himself. Kibosh, standing next to him, nodded in quiet assertion.

"You did your best to find her. If you couldn't, nobody could."

Thunderclap's face clouded. He and Jasper had searched every corner of the outpost with no luck. Summer was gone and there seemed to be only two conclusions: either she had been sucked up into a time tornado, or the Ziffians . . . He couldn't finish the terrible thought. Swallowing, he looked back up at the ceiling and steeled his resolve. He would make them pay. Before they could take him down he would make sure of that.

Suddenly the dome cracked and a red light burst through. Students scampered to avoid the falling debris as the Ziffian lasers finally accomplished their goal. Horrible sounds escaped from the alien throats, their shouts of triumph as they tore through the ceiling.

Just as the first of the terrible creatures entered the demolished room, a crimson streak flew down, carrying a huge brass machine. Thunderclap boggled. It was Summer! And she was wearing . . .

"Truehart's cape," Kibosh breathed in awe.

At that moment the aliens let out a cry of alarm. The sounds of hundreds of heavy clanking feet were marching, advancing on the aliens from behind. If their monstrous eyes were capable of registering terror, they did at this moment. A unified scream of rage escaped their sinewy throats.

"Look!" someone shouted. The heroes turned and saw the source of the aliens' fear. The Elite Guard, flanked by the Cryogenic Crusaders, had returned. Summer wasted no time. She flew up into the sky like a crimson bolt and, signaling the Crusaders, activated the strange-looking brass contraption.

The crowd watched as the aliens screamed and sizzled, seeming to melt before their eyes. The machine Summer held emitted a blast of green energy that, when it hit the creatures, caused them immeasurable damage. Within seconds, the entire alien army had shrunk down to the size of small trees. Kibosh grinned as the Cryogenic Crusaders let out a shout and unsheathed their glittering swords.

"A fair fight!" The massive boy rubbed his hands together. "Let's get 'em!"

...22 THE AFTERMATH

THE battle was over in a matter of minutes. The aliens, their powers still active but much reduced, were soon overcome by the heroic assault. Summer was incredible, delivering power-packed punches and sending sizzling energy bolts into the villainous foe. Before the attack she had paused to enhance the powers of the other heroes, giving them each twice their normal strength!

After the aliens who had survived were rounded up, the Cryogenic Crusaders pointed the tips of their icy swords at the defeated beasts. The aliens, seeming to have experienced this once before in the distant past, hissed and howled menacingly, recognizing their fate. Suddenly the Crusaders let out a unified cry.

"Activate!"

Icy blue beams shot from the extended weapons and hit the aliens with tremendous force. In moments the creatures were frozen into a sleepless slumber, their eyes wide and blinking, trapped in individual coffins of ice.

Thunderclap ran to Summer, and grabbed her in a long embrace.

Summer, blushing fiercely, hugged him back. When they finally separated they felt a bit awkward. Archie cleared his throat and grinned.

"Wow, where did you get the cool cape?"

Summer laughed, looking down at the beautiful crimson folds. Then, thinking about how she had come by it, she suddenly remembered something she had to do. She gathered her friends together and told them about Tommy and his sacrifice.

The others were incredulous at the news. Most believed that Tommy's heroic act was genuine, and accepted his apology. A few others were still skeptical, having experienced the other side of his personality.

Summer turned to Thunderclap with a thoughtful expression.

"Archie, there is something I need to apologize for too." She turned and walked back to the remains of the outpost, making her way to the relatively undamaged Healing Wing.

Her dad and Betty were sitting beside Dennis, who was sitting up, listening to what had happened in the battle outside. He turned and looked at Summer as she walked through the door, his smile disappearing. Summer approached his bedside.

"Dennis, I want to apologize. I haven't been very nice, not very much of the kind of big sister I guess I should get ready to be." Dennis looked down at his bedsheets.

Summer continued. "I guess what I'm asking for is a second chance."

Reaching to her shoulders, Summer unclasped the magnificent cape and, as she removed it, felt the surge of power melt away. Folding it gently, she handed it to Dennis. "This is for you."

Summer couldn't see his expression as Dennis held the cape in his small hands, his head bowed. Suddenly he lifted his eyes to hers, and they were shining with happiness.

"Thank you, Summer."

Summer smiled broadly as she felt Jasper's and Betty's arms around her shoulders. Maybe Dennis wasn't such a bad kid after all.

Suddenly footsteps rang out in the corridor. Thunderclap entered the room, breathless, his face flushed.

"Hurry!" he gasped. "You gotta get out of here, there's a time tornado!"

The others looked at each other in alarm. Jasper picked Dennis up out of the bed and rushed Betty and Summer out the door. As they sped down the hall, a booming noise swept through the building and the walls began to shimmer.

"Too late!" Thunderclap yelled as the massive tornado touched down and removed the entire Healing Wing from the present time.

. . . 23 A NEW BEGINNING

SUMMER grasped the udder of the uncooperative cow with two fingers. Even though her dad had shown her how it was supposed to be done, she still managed to get most of the milk on the floor instead of inside the metal bucket.

Bess, who waited patiently for Summer to figure out what she was doing, let out a low "mooooo." Summer grinned.

It had been three months since they had arrived in the Old West. They were in the

Conejo Valley, a small Western town that would in one hundred twenty years or so eventually become the Thousand Oaks that she knew. Shortly after they had arrived, Jasper discovered the remains of the rocket, helped by an eyewitness who complained that it had materialized on top of his barn. They had spent the first several days salvaging what they could from the wreck, and Summer had been delighted to find that Clocksprocket was still magnetized to the wall in her cabin, where she had left him.

She pushed back the bonnet she wore, and lifted her head to feel the cool breeze that drifted into the barn.

Betty and her dad had gotten married at the local church a few days later. It had been a very happy ceremony and Betty had even made sure that when she tossed the bouquet, it "accidentally" landed straight in Summer's lap. She had giggled. Marriage was still a long way off, but she and Thunderclap had exchanged embarrassed glances.

Her dad had contacted a man named H. G. Wells who lived in England and had written a book about time machines. The man wrote back that he was eager to meet with him, and that building an actual working time machine might even be possible!

Suddenly a swooping noise caught her attention. With a loud, joyful *whoop* Dennis flew down to land in front of her, spooking the cow.

"Be careful, she won't give me any milk if she's scared." Summer patted Bessie's side comfortingly. Dennis chuckled. Summer noticed that he was wearing the clothes that Betty had bought for him at the local mercantile, a cowboy hat and boots, with Truehart's cape flowing out behind him.

"Mom says that it is time for dinner. You coming?"

"Yeah." Summer gave one more halfhearted tug on the udder and sighed. She grabbed the bucket and stood up.

"If you wanna use the cape after dinner, you can." Dennis looked up at Summer, who smiled back down at him.

"Nah, you go ahead." She tousled his hair. "I know you are still 'breaking it in.'"

The small boy looked up at her adoringly and grinned. "You know what?"

"What?"

"Last one to the kitchen is a rotten Ziffian." And before Summer could say a word the little boy had taken off, flying like a bullet to the doorway of their small farmhouse. Summer smiled to herself as she walked slowly back, gazing at the beautiful sunset that was reflecting off the pink clouds.

When she entered the small, oil lamp–lit kitchen and sat down, her dad, wearing a plaid shirt and suspenders, cleared his throat. Betty smiled cryptically and took a seat beside him.

Dennis left off eyeing the fluffy buttermilk biscuits long enough to see that his parents were about to make some kind of announcement. Jasper held Betty's hand and gazed happily around the table. Thunderclap sat next to Summer and raised his eyebrows expectantly. Jasper couldn't contain himself any longer. With an excited grin he blurted out, "Betty and I have an announcement to make."

Summer's heart flip-flopped when she heard the words. She knew something big was coming.

"We're PREGNANT!"

baby

PHOTO: NANCY LETHCOE

ABOUT THE AUTHOR

JASON LETHCOE has worked as an animator and story artist for several Hollywood studios including Disney, Warner Bros., Dreamworks, and Universal Studios. He currently resides in Newbury Park, California, with his wife, Nancy, and their three children, Emily, Alex, and Olivia Rose. When not writing on *The Moon*, his thirty-foot sailboat, you may catch a glimpse of Jason and his fourteen-pound eyeball at the local bowling alley.